A BROWNSTONE RESPONSE

A BROWNSTONE RESPONSE

ALISON BROWNSTONE™ BOOK NINE

JUDITH BERENS   MARTHA CARR   MICHAEL ANDERLE

DISRUPTIVE IMAGINATION®

Copyright © 2019 Judith Berens, Martha Carr and Michael Anderle
Cover by Fantasy Book Design
Cover copyright © LMBPN Publishing
A Michael Anderle Production

LMBPN Publishing
PMB 196, 2540 South Maryland Pkwy
Las Vegas, NV 89109

First US edition, June 2019
Version 1.06, November 2020
Print ISBN: 978-1-64202-783-9

A BROWNSTONE RESPONSE TEAM

Thanks to the JIT Readers

Dave Hicks
Daniel Weigert
Diane L. Smith
Shari Regan
Jeff Eaton
Nicole Emens
Paul Westman
Peter Manis
Jeff Goode
John Ashmore
Misty Roa

If we've missed anyone, please let us know!

Editor
SkyHunter Editing Team

From Martha

To everyone who still believes in magic
and all the possibilities that holds.
To all the readers who make this
entire ride so much fun.
And to my son, Louie and so many wonderful friends who
remind me all the time of what
really matters and how wonderful
life can be in any given moment.

From Michael

To Family, Friends and
Those Who Love
To Read.
May We All Enjoy Grace
To Live The Life We Are
Called.

CHAPTER ONE

Alison kept her face blank as she stared at the scarred man in the ill-fitting suit in front of her desk. Glaring or scowling at him wouldn't help her understand the situation, and a mixture of curiosity and irritation fueled her attention.

If this is another stunt by Rasila, I'll have to seriously kick her ass. She knows enough about the underworld to pull off something like this.

It had been a couple of months since she had fought the other Drow princess. That might have been enough time for her to cook up a new scheme.

When Ava had explained who had called and asked to meet with her, Alison had thought it was some kind of joke or mistaken identity, especially since the caller had insisted it had to be that day. Now, however, she had an actual leader of a local Eastern Union gang in her office.

Is this some sort of feeble assassination attempt? If it were, you'd think he would have taken his shot already. He looks nervous, but there are a lot of reasons why that could be.

"Call me Andrei," the man suggested, and a faint Russian accent seasoned his words. "I want us to be friends, and I have all my friends call me Andrei. I will call you whatever you want."

"Call me Alison." She nodded slowly. "And to be clear, you do know who I am, right? This isn't something where you looked me up on the Internet and somehow failed to hear anything else about my time in Seattle?"

Andrei looked confused. "I don't understand."

"I find it hard to believe someone like you wants to be friends with me." She let a frown slip through. "Considering my previous experiences with the Eastern Union."

"Yes, yes. You are Alison Brownstone." He stared at her for a moment. "The Dark Princess. Everyone in Seattle knows who you are, especially in the Eastern Union. You have killed many of our men. It would be hard to not know who you are in our line of work."

"By your line of work, you mean organized crime." She unfolded her hands. "I don't understand why an Eastern Union leader would come asking me for help. You're obviously aware of how much damage I've done to the Eastern Union groups in this city."

Andrei gave her a curt nod. "Yes, I know all that. It's why I've always told my guys, 'You don't anger Alison Brownstone. If you do, you're on your own.' My guys…we don't do trafficking either. I know you don't like that. We never did it, but I told the guys who wanted to start that we wouldn't. It's too much trouble."

Too much trouble but not it's immoral?

Alison scoffed. "You're still a gangster. Merely being a restrained gangster doesn't make you a saint."

"We help provide products to people who want them." He swallowed and adjusted his tie. "I won't claim I'm not a criminal, but I've tried to lead my guys in a way that doesn't cause trouble for you and yours."

"Okay, I have trouble processing this still." She leaned back in her chair and frowned. "My assistant said you specifically asked for a meeting because you needed to hire my security company ASAP—as in today." She gestured around them. "You didn't mention on the phone who you were, but she recognized your name. I kept telling myself, 'This is some other random guy with the same name as an Eastern Union leader.'"

Andrei managed a weak grin. "I'm sure there are others with my name. I won't deny that. But I won't deny who and what I am, and I need your help because of who you are and your experience with the Eastern Union."

Alison shook her head. "Just because your little crew hasn't personally pissed me off doesn't mean you can hire me. I'm not some for-hire muscle for gangsters to send at their enemies. If that was your big plan, give it up."

The mobster's smile disappeared, and Andrei sighed. "It's true I need you to help me with my enemies."

"Then you should get up and leave." She pointed to her closed door. "I'm not a paid killer. I'm a security contractor."

He raised his palm placatingly. "It's not what you think. I don't care if anyone's killed, but they've taken something important, and I need you to get it back. I think few could do it other than you."

"I don't care about your gangster turf wars." Alison

narrowed her eyes. "Unless you involve innocents, and if that happens, you'll all pay."

"But they have involved an innocent." Andrei took several deep breaths. "They have kidnapped my wife Katya."

Alison opened her mouth to release another rude comment before she closed it slowly and nodded. She considered her response for a few seconds. "I see. And what do they want for her return?"

"For me to leave town, along with certain caches of money and weapons I've stored. I'm fine doing it, but these men who have done this have no honor. I can't take a chance of leaving only for her to die." His nostrils flared. "And if I do, these honorless men will be stronger. They will simply do it again."

"Why not go to the cops?" She shrugged. "The Seattle PD won't look the other way simply because she's a mobster's wife."

"If I knew exactly where she was, I might consider it, but it's still a bad idea." Andrei shook his head. "Involving the police would only show more weakness and cause more instability. More will suffer. I don't want a war. I merely want my wife back."

"How would me being involved not destabilize things? Things tend to get messy when I have to knock on doors."

He gave her long, penetrating look. "It's been hard to get things balanced in this area, but now we're all in orbit around one dark star. You, Dark Princess. You're not considered truly part of the police's world, even if you help them. Many in the underworld think of you as part of ours."

She snorted. "I'm not a criminal. I'm a security contractor. I don't go looking for fights with gangsters."

Andrei nodded slowly. "You're a woman who rules through strength. You are a woman who destroys your enemies when they wrong you. You're more like us than you think." His eyes filled with pride.

Alison's face twitched. "I protect people."

"Whether you believe what I say or not, that's the truth for us in the Eastern Union. And if you're involved, I can explain it away as someone violating the rules the Dark Princess supports. There will be no turf war, then, and the status quo will be maintained." He shrugged. "No more innocents get hurt."

"Or I could end up igniting a huge turf war. What about you? How do I know you won't go after the other group? You probably hope I take out a few people along the way, and then you can get revenge for your wife."

He sighed. "I'm through."

"Through?"

"I have money. I don't need more." He looked at his rough hands. "My wife has asked to have children for years, and I've said no because I thought it wasn't safe enough for us. Once I have her back, I'll leave this area. I will do something else. I'm tired of my life. I'm simply a man and can never have the power of someone like you. Why do I struggle so much for it when I joined the Union first for money? I have more money than my parents would ever know what to do with."

Alison took a deep breath. "If you plan to leave anyway, there's even more reason for you to agree to a swap."

Andrei raised his head. "No. It's as I told you. If I

trusted them to release her, I would accept, but I've dealt with these men before. They are cruel and look for weakness. They have killed hostages. They are despicable."

Gangsters calling other gangsters despicable. Fine. Let's make sure this is for real.

She made a few careful movements with her hands and chanted a quick spell. A white orb formed in front of her.

"This is a very simple truth detection spell," she explained. "I'll ask you a few questions. If you lie about any of them, we're done here. Understand?"

He swallowed and nodded, his gaze fixed on the orb.

"Has your wife really been kidnapped by another Eastern Union group?" Alison asked.

"Yes," Andrei answered and stared at the orb. It remained the same color.

"Do you truly believe they won't let your wife go if you comply with their demands?"

"Yes."

Alison watched the orb. It remained white.

She took a deep breath. "And will you leave town and crime if I save your wife?"

Andrei locked eyes with her. "Yes."

"One last question. You haven't been contacted by any outside people, especially a woman, and told to contact me?"

Confusion swallowed the apprehension on Andrei's face. "No, not at all."

The orb hasn't changed. Rasila isn't sitting behind every shadow, after all.

Alison gave a faint nod and released the magic fueling the spell. "I'll talk to my staff, and I'll let you know in a few hours. If we agree to do this, we'll use the minimum force necessary to recover your wife. I won't clean out an Eastern Union group only for another to grow stronger in the vacuum. It's like you said—stability." She took a deep breath. "So, tell me a little more about who you think kidnapped your wife and what kind of defenses they might have. Also, I'll need a picture."

Thirty minutes later, Alison sat at the head of her conference room table. Hana, Tahir, Drysi, and Mason were scattered around the table. Ava sat near the front, her tablet in her hand while she took notes. Sonya wasn't present, as she currently ran support for an escort mission performed by Jerry's team.

"So, there you have it." Alison finished explaining the general situation. "It does seem like we have an actual criminal kidnapping situation. I'm not crazy about working for a criminal, but I also don't like the idea that other criminals think they can simply snatch whoever they want. From what I've seen of the Union, their wives aren't involved much in their actual criminal activities."

Tahir's face became a mask of incredulity. "She might not be involved in his criminal activities, but she most undoubtedly knows what he is. That at least speaks to some contradiction of her relative innocence." He scoffed.

"True enough," she replied. "But I still don't want the Eastern Union to think it's okay to kidnap people. I'm not a priest or a philosopher. I'm not here to make too many fine judgments about the morality of being married to a criminal."

Mason frowned. "Are we really convinced that getting the police involved would cause a turf war? This seems like a police job."

She shrugged. "My instincts actually tell me yes. Not only that, the police might take too long to resolve the situation. I made a quick call to an informant to ask him a couple of questions about the group that kidnapped Andrei's wife. They are a smaller group but they are known for cruelty, and they've tried to keep a low profile because of me."

"And you're sure that you getting involved won't cause trouble?" The life wizard's brow raised. "There's no point in doing this if we ignite a gang war. Saving one woman so many other people can get hurt isn't good math."

"Brownstone Security hasn't started a gang war with everything else we've done to Eastern Union operations. I don't see why a restricted-scope rescue mission would do more."

Drysi chuckled. "I bet you these bloody fools will hide even more after Alison does her thing. And as far as the rest of the world is concerned, she and her Dad led a tidy little clean up in Vancouver."

"That was a couple of months ago," he replied.

"It doesn't change anything." Drysi nodded curtly. "A lot of the bloody bastards out there are afraid Alison's still on the warpath. The news didn't make it clear what happened in Vancouver, other than Brownstone and friends showed up and stopped some dangerous artifact from vomiting monsters."

Would the world feel differently if they knew that we were up there to settle a personal score? I don't know. The Seventh Order had hurt many people, and if they'd succeeded, they could have hurt far more, but it's probably for the best that people don't know everything that happened there.

Alison stomach tightened. It might have also been better if the world understood that Myna had died helping save human lives. The US and Canadian governments had very particular spins they wanted put on the events in Vancouver. At the time, Alison had agreed, but now, she wasn't so sure.

"Alison?" Mason's voice cut through her thoughts.

She blinked and looked at him. "Huh?"

"We lost you there for a minute." He looked at her with concern.

"Sorry, I got distracted." She shook her head. "Sorry."

Ava continued to tap away in silence as she recorded her notes.

Hana leaned over the table, rested her head in the palm of her hand, and supported her arm with her elbow. "I don't care about the reasons. If it involves punching Eastern Union guys, I'm for it. They're all garbage. If this guy actually cares about his wife, then fine, we can help him out. It's a nice excuse to do that, and if this woman isn't so bad, great. That makes it even better. I think we need to grab some of these guys every once in a while and throw them up against the wall as a reminder not to mess with the Dark Princess."

"This could get dangerous," Mason observed, his arms folded. "I'm not saying it's too much, only that we might want to keep it to the primary team to cut down on the

9

risk of casualties, especially given the client and the nature of the mission."

Alison nodded. "Agreed." She surveyed the table. "I don't want to do this if any of you have strong objections. Even if I went alone, it would have implications for the rest of you."

"There's no way I'll let you go alone, A," the bodyguard replied.

Hana shrugged. "I'm ready for punching. Maybe a little clawing, too."

Drysi grinned. "I won't lie. Hana's right. Beating gangsters feels bloody good no matter the reason."

Alison looked from the Welsh witch to the nine-tailed fox. Both shrugged with playful grins on their faces.

"I won't even be on site, so it's not like it's a particular risk to me," Tahir commented.

"All right, then. I guess Brownstone Security's doing a little rescue operation." She turned toward the infomancer. "We know the who, and now we need to know the where. From what Andrei told me, her kidnappers have access to a cell that's been warded, so simple tracking won't work. Let me know if you can figure out something or if I need to have him fork over personal items so we can try a directional tracking spell."

Tahir looked offended. "That won't be necessary. If I can't deal with these Eastern Union systems in the next couple of hours and find her, I might as well quit."

CHAPTER TWO

The infomancer stepped into Alison's office a half-hour later, a far more smug look of satisfaction on his face than normal. "It's hard to believe these gangsters hold such sway when their cybersecurity practices are so pathetic. You wouldn't even need me. Sonya could handle them. Not that she's not talented."

Alison raised an eyebrow. "Oh? I take it you know where Katya is? I expected to have to use a directional tracking spell."

He waved a hand dismissively. "It was easy. All it took was a simple penetration of their systems and I was able to identify the phone numbers associated with the relevant men. Then it was merely a matter of checking on them and their current locations. Your informant was right. There is a rather noticeable magical block around a group of phones associated with the targets in a particular location."

"That could be a coincidence," she suggested. "Maybe they want to have somewhere safe for other reasons."

"Perhaps, but they are still the relevant members." Tahir

shrugged. "If it's the wrong location, you can interrogate them until they give you the new location. I doubt any Eastern Union faction has several different anti-magic rooms."

"Good point. So where is the likely place?"

"It's a penthouse condo near downtown," he explained. "Ironically, it's not all that far from your condo building. It's within walking distance, actually, if you were still living there."

Alison chuckled. "I guess I started moving too early."

Her and Mason had finally chosen their new rental only a few weeks prior, but it had been a slow process to transfer her possessions to the new house and secure it with the necessary wards and glyphs. She hadn't sold her condo because she wasn't sure what she would do with it.

"The penthouse, huh?" she murmured. "I don't think this has to be complicated."

"We're rescuing the wife of a gangster from other gangsters. I think it's already complicated."

"That's a good point, but it's not some fortified warehouse or weird ultra-magic mansion." She stood. "I'll hit them hard and fast, rescue the woman, and be in and out before they even know what the hell is going on or can get reinforcements."

She'd briefly considered moving into this very building when she first came to Seattle, but there was something about the vibe that didn't work for her. Alison took a deep breath as she stared at the tower of windows that loomed over her. Maybe she had sensed it had scum living there—or, at least, more scum than usual.

I wonder if any gangsters live in my old building? Maybe Ryan's secretly a gangster, and he's been lying this entire time.

"Can everyone hear me?" she murmured, hoping not to draw attention from anyone walking up the street. "And you're all in position? If anything goes bad, the most important thing is to make sure the woman gets out. I can handle myself against the Union. Understood?"

"Understood," Mason replied through her receiver. "We're in the 'copter and ready to go on your orders. If they try to move her anywhere in the city, we'll be able to catch up."

"I don't like this plan," Hana muttered. "I'm supposed to be there punching Eastern Union guys, not waiting to fly off to some secondary place and maybe punching guys. You should have taken me with you."

"The point isn't to punch guys," her boss explained. "The point is to save Katya."

The fox grumbled a few more complaints under her breath.

"Drysi, are you in position?" Alison asked.

"I'm parked up the street in the SUV," she replied. "I'll drive up once you start the op, but I agree with Hana. This is boring. I'm the driver now? At least Mason gets to be the pilot."

"You don't even know how to fly a helicopter."

"That doesn't make it less boring."

Alison sighed. "I'm sorry that not every job can be action-packed. Tahir, status report."

"No unusual activity on drones," he reported. "They still

have the blinds closed in the penthouse. Thermal readings indicate multiple people inside, and there's at least one person who I'm fairly certain is tied to a chair judging by their thermal silhouette. I count seven other humanoid signatures inside. Based on the blueprints I pulled, the woman's most likely in the master bedroom. If you enter from the street-side window, you'll be in the dining room. You can go straight to the living room and take a hallway to the right to reach the bedroom."

"Okay." She craned her head to look upward. "I'll go up there, grab her, and land. I won't be all that fast if I try to carry another person, but mostly, I simply have to fall slowly enough that we both don't die."

Drysi laughed. "Impressive, Alison."

"Hey, I can't be great at everything." She rolled her eyes, but she did wonder if a more experienced Drow could pull that off. While she knew a few telekinesis spells, she found them hard to combine when in flight. It was more a failure of technique than power.

I'm strong, but I still have a lot to learn.

A passing man glanced her way and muttered something about rude people who talked on the phone without having the decency to at least hold a phone.

Better that than he realizes I'm about to start a major raid and calls the cops to complicate things. Okay, I have to make sure there's no falling glass. I need to be careful about this.

"If she's not there, you'll have to move your asses to the new location so they can't run," Alison explained.

"Just do your thing, A," Mason suggested. "We have your back."

"Okay, I'll get started." She extended her shadow wings.

Several people stopped and looked her way, some curious and some afraid. A few retrieved their phones to start filming. A small boy's eyes widened with delight. He tugged on his mother's hand and pointed at the half-Drow.

One man rolled his eyes and continued walking. "Show off," he muttered.

Alison elevated smoothly and soared upward. Five stories. Ten stories. Twenty stories. Forty stories. She reached the top floor. If the enemy had cameras, they would now see a Drow princess hovering outside their secret penthouse prison.

Hello, boys.

She floated in front of the window and extended a shadow blade. With a quick motion, she stabbed forward to pierce the window and the blinds and dragged the blade up. She kicked out with her leg to keep the window from falling outward as she finished carving an opening. A few pieces of the blinds fluttered down but no glass.

With a deep breath, she pushed forward. The glass fell into the apartment and cracked as it struck the hardwood of the dining room floor.

Six gangsters stood in the living room, their faces masks of shock as she made her appearance through the window. Piles of chips and playing cards lay on the table.

"Sorry to interrupt your game." Alison dropped into the dining room. Glass crunched beneath her boot heels. "I'm Alison Brownstone, and I'm here for Katya. Hand her over."

The men recovered in seconds and leapt behind the couches while they drew their guns. Clicks and slaps followed. Several full ejected magazines skittered across the ground.

Swapping to anti-magics, huh?

She layered shields over herself and dropped the wings before she crouched and channeled power to her legs. The shadow blade faded, and a blue-white baton of energy appeared in her right hand.

The problem with being powerful was that everyone always believed that having power made it easy for someone to defeat their enemies. While that was true, it also made it difficult to accomplish it without killing them. She wasn't always in a position to know for certain whether ruthless extermination was warranted or desirable. In this situation, she wasn't sure if killing any of the Eastern Union would actually cause trouble, but she didn't want to take the chance.

"This doesn't involve you, Dark Princess," one of the gangsters shouted. "This is all Eastern Union business."

Alison sighed. She raised her free arm, still crouched. "Come on. Do you really think that line will work on me? If I'm here, I have a good reason to be here."

"But we didn't mess with any of your people," the gangster growled. "You shouldn't be here."

"You know what? I don't have time for this garbage." She released her pent-up energy and launched herself toward the wall. A shadow line flung to another wall enabled her to swing through the living room with her conjured stun baton in hand.

The gangsters turned, but it was too late as she had already released her line and barreled toward them.

She brought the stun baton down on the first man. He

jerked and his pistol fell free, and he twitched as he sagged. She shoved her hand out and delivered a stun bolt to the next closest man. He groaned and catapulted away to land with a loud thud.

A spin ended with two other men down before she thrust behind her to strike another gangster in the head. A roundhouse kick connected with the final opponent's head with a loud crunch. He hurtled over the couch, unconscious, and blood spewed from his nose.

"Tahir, talk to me," Alison murmured. "Wait. I only count six guys. Didn't you say there were seven?"

"There's someone in the room with the woman," the infomancer reported.

She winced. "Damn. Not fast enough." Irritated, she jammed her stun rod into a stirring gangster and marched down the hallway, her expression hard. The door to the master bedroom stood open.

Cautiously, she turned the corner. A gangster in a tracksuit stood with his gun to the head of a plain brown-haired woman with glasses. She was tied to a wooden chair with thick rope. Her face matched the picture of Katya that Andrei had sent them, but her cheeks were red from obvious tears, and her right cheek and eye were swollen and blackened.

Alison had been surprised when she received the picture. Katya wasn't the hot young trophy wife she had expected of an Eastern Union gangster.

"Put the gun down," she ordered. "I'm already pissed that you beat her up."

The man gritted his teeth. "The bitch bit Gregor. She needed to understand her place."

She bit one of them? Good for her.

"You're really trying my patience." she sighed. "I haven't killed anyone in this condo yet, but if you harm her, I might have to reconsider that."

He swallowed. "You're lying. The Dark Princess' rage is legendary. You probably butchered all of them."

Alison scoffed. "Seriously? If you're worried I'm a deadly killer, then pissing me off is about the last thing you should do, asshole." She released her stun baton. "Do you really think you'll win against a woman who fought a Mountain Strider?"

His hand shook and he backed away from Katya to aim his gun at Alison. "You're not a monster. You're not Baba Yaga. You're simply some half-elf."

When she heard that, she regretted that her nickname had ended up as Dark Princess. Being called the same name as the legendary Russian witch would have been far more interesting. For the first time, she could relate to Hana's desire for a cool nickname.

Maybe there's a real Baba Yaga out there. Ha. If vampires were real, there would probably already be a scary bitch with that nickname.

"Yeah, here's the thing," she pointed out with an indifferent shrug. "I'm not Baba Yaga because I'm real, and she isn't. More importantly, I'm right here in front of you. Drop your damned gun."

Her adversary jerked his hand to the side and now aimed the gun at Katya. "Back off, Dark Princess. Your fancy magic won't do anything if I blow her brains out."

Alison raised her left arm.

The other man frowned. "What are you doing?"

"Distracting you, idiot." She thrust her other palm forward and summoned a blue-white stun bolt.

It struck her opponent in the chest, and he jerked back and careened into the wall. He slid down and drool seeped from the side of his mouth.

She marched over to the man and kicked his gun beneath the bed before she channeled energy into a short shadow blade a few inches in length. With this, she sliced through Katya's bonds.

"Come on." She held her hand out. "I want to get you away from this place as soon as possible, so...uh, we'll go out the window."

The woman stood and rubbed her wrists. "The window?" She blinked, clearly confused. "Like with a parachute?"

Alison extended her wings. "We'll simply float to the ground with magic, and I'll have a friend waiting to pick us up."

Katya looked unconvinced but she nodded and nibbled her lip.

The women headed back to the broken window. Alison raised her hands and two shadow tendrils emerged and wound around the Russian to pull the woman close.

"Ready?" she asked.

"As ready as I could for something so absurd."

Alison dropped backward out the window. She fell several yards before she flipped and funneled more magic into her wings. Gravity's relentless control still tugged, but now, she could circle as she descended with Katya against her in a gentle glide rather than a fall.

The woman's eyes widened, and she shook her head. "This is not how I thought this would end."

Their leisurely descent was captured by dozens of people who aimed their cameras skyward. It wasn't every day you saw someone with tenebrous wings carrying a woman down from a condo.

The SUV came into view. The driver's side, passenger, and back doors were already open. Drysi stood near the front with her hand in her jacket, ready to whip out an enchanted dagger or gun as necessary.

"How are we doing, Tahir?" Alison asked.

Katya looked at her but understanding dawned on her face.

"They tried to send a message, but I blocked their phones," he replied. "And I don't see any unusual vehicles."

"Good. It's nice when something goes the way you expect." She touched down beside the SUV, set her passenger down, and pointed to the open back door.

The Russian hurried inside and slammed the door closed behind her. Drysi gave her boss a polite nod and slid into the driver's seat. Alison walked around and hopped into the passenger seat.

Drysi eased out into the traffic. "You're the only one who got to have any fun, Alison."

"Seriously unfair," Hana grumbled through the receiver.

The half-Drow looked over her shoulder at Katya, whose expression was a mixture of gratitude and relief. "You and Hana will have to punch gangsters some other time."

CHAPTER THREE

Andrei pulled Katya into a tight embrace as they stood in front of the Brownstone Security building with Alison. The team had taken her there on the assumption that the Eastern Union gang wouldn't dare attack them directly. After the failed dark wizard attack, no one believed a direct assault on Brownstone Security made any sense at all.

The Russian gangster ran his hand gingerly over Katya's face. "I'm sorry. It's all my fault they did this to you. If I could take it all on myself, I would."

Katya shook her head. "I'm safe now. It's all over."

Mason cleared his throat. "I can heal those injuries for you. It won't hurt."

She looked at her husband, and he nodded.

"I need to talk to the Dar—Alison," he murmured. "Let the wizard heal you." He kissed her forehead and walked over to Alison. Katya headed to Mason, a grateful smile on her face.

He might be a criminal, but he does love his wife. This wasn't a bad job at all.

Andrei sighed. "Thank you again, Dark Princess," he murmured, his voice low. "I don't know if I would have been able to rescue her myself, and I'm not so sure some of my men would have been willing to risk themselves."

"What now?" Alison asked. Even if the man hadn't lied in her office, that didn't mean he couldn't change his mind.

"I'll be leaving," he replied. "My second-in-command will take over, but I don't know how much gratitude he might extend to you, even though I've made it clear you helped. I'm sorry."

She shrugged. "I'm not all that worried about favors from the Eastern Union. No offense. I don't need them."

"No, of course you don't." He looked over his shoulder and watched as Mason raised his wand and chanted the healing spell. "Everyone fears you in the underworld, like a story you might tell a child to get him to behave."

Katya's bruises faded.

"Good. That should help cut down on the number of stupid things they do—like kidnapping wives or generally being cruel assholes." Alison shook her head. "I came to Seattle as a security contractor, not a bounty hunter or vigilante. I don't want to get involved in this crap."

"You don't understand. Fear is currency. There are few people more powerful than you in this city. You should use that currency." His expression turned gloomy. "Use it to your advantage and the benefit of all of us."

She frowned. "To do what, exactly? I don't need more money or power. I won't start a protection racket against the other guys running protection rackets."

"There is one constant in life, whether it's magicals or non-magicals. There are always criminals. There is always darkness. Do you agree?"

"I don't argue the point but that's why you need people like me." She shrugged. "I don't follow what you're getting at. I want the underworld afraid of me, but I won't try to cash in from that."

Andrei leaned forward, an almost reverent look on his face. "History teaches us that a benevolent but strong ruler can bring peace. If there will always be an underworld, why not a queen of the underworld? One who could stop the darkest excesses. You can't eliminate crime, so why not control it? Save wives and save innocents."

Alison snorted and resisted pointing out that men weren't the only criminals she had dealt with. "I'm only one woman. If the police, feds, and bounty hunters— including my father—can't eliminate crime, I won't be able to. It'd be beyond arrogant to believe I could."

The Russian shook his head. "I mean only in this city. There have been no queens of the underworld, but there have been queens of countries and cities." He sighed and desperation replaced the resignation on his face. "You could make a difference. You're already a princess among your own people so why not become a queen among others?"

She shook her head firmly. "I already make a difference and I know my limits. I'll continue to do what I have been doing—dealing with people when they get out of hand. I don't think me doing anything else would be a good thing."

Andrei nodded respectfully. "Maybe it is good that you Brownstones have such power but you don't wish to use it.

It still surprises me to this day that your father has focused his efforts on running a restaurant. He could have been a god. I suppose you follow in this path. Still..." He sucked in a breath.

"Still what?"

He sighed and turned away. "Both worlds would be better if those who didn't want power were the ones who wielded it, but we live in an imperfect world." He stuck his hands in the pockets of his suit and walked toward his now healed wife.

Queen of the Underworld and Queen of the Drow? Yeah, no thanks. I'll pass.

Alison smiled inwardly but the frustration melted away as Andrei took Katya's hand. The man might have been a thug, but he had found something more important to him and maybe, just maybe, his children would be able to move on from his legacy.

I can't change the world, but I can change people, one at a time.

Alison summoned a hasty sound-dampening bubble before she stepped past the crystalline Halican bouncers in front of the True Portal.

It might be too much to say she had become a regular of the club, but as she entered and noticed a familiar Arpak woman dancing in the corner and several equally as familiar drunken elves mixing with a group of human break dancers, she smiled.

I remember the first time I came to this place, and those

bouncers acted like I wasn't good enough to come in here. Now, if I don't see certain people, I wonder if they're okay and I don't even know their names.

Her spell protected her ears from the techno assault that blasted from the speakers, but the heavy bass vibrated through the floor and rattled her body. She headed toward the stairs leading to the second-story landing.

Vincent is nothing if not consistent. I'm surprised he doesn't find a new club to hang out at now and again. The guy's overly confident no one will try to assassinate him.

The man never made it clear who might be guarding him or what kind of defenses he had available. Either he was the greatest bluffer in the world, or he had a reasonable expectation that it would take a major effort to eliminate him.

Before Alison reached the stairs, a tall man in a very out-of-place bright yellow zoot suit gestured for her to join him on the dance floor. She offered him a smile and waved him off. He shrugged and winked before he continued to dance alone.

There are so many people here having a good time. Maybe I should come here with Mason sometime simply to relax rather than talk to Vincent. But I don't like the idea of my fun place also being where I usually meet an informant.

She climbed the stairs slowly, her gaze fixed on the dancers as she ran her hand along the smooth railing. Familiar. That's what the club felt like, as did the Brownstone Building, Café Artemis, and so many other places there. It'd been a tumultuous year, but Seattle wasn't merely a city she had moved to anymore. It was her home, as much her home as her dad's house in L.A. or the School of Necessary Magic had been.

In a few more steps, she crested the stairs. Vincent sat at a table in his more traditional purple suit with layers of gold chains around his neck. Sometimes, she wondered if he purposefully wanted to look sleazy or if he honestly thought he looked slick in that kind of outfit. Or it might have been a deliberate attempt at deceit to make people like her underestimate him.

He inclined his head toward an empty chair across from him. She headed that way and released her sound-dampening bubble. The full riot of techno infused with a few shrill Oriceran flutes erupted around her before she stepped into a new oasis of quiet that surrounded the table. The magic tingled slightly.

Alison dropped into the seat and folded her arms. "Nice night."

"It is, isn't it?" The informer tapped his phone, which lay on the table. "I'm curious, Dark Princess. You paid me already for information I haven't actually given you. Once you sent the payment, I knew you would come, but that's not usually how you work—or even how I work." He picked up his martini, which was currently an inky purple.

"I had a good week. Maybe I feel generous." She gestured toward the drink. "Did someone just lie to you?"

"A few minutes ago. A Wood Elf who should have known better." Vincent sighed. "His loss. I'm willing to tolerate certain lies, but this one pushed it too far."

"I'm curious. Does it taste different when the spell activates?"

He took a small sip of his drink and shook his head.

"There's no reason to waste a perfectly good drink, and I don't want to train my palate to enjoy lies, do I?"

"You care that much about lies?"

"Of course." Vincent licked his lips. "I love the truth. For one thing, it's very valuable. I've never lied to you, now, have I?"

Alison chuckled. "Okay, I hadn't thought of it that way, but good point."

The informer set the drink now. "I assume your generosity doesn't simply represent a bonus?"

She shook her head. "I've had some of my people and other informants ask around, but I wanted to visit you to get a good read on the current Eastern Union situation."

His lips curled into a grin. "You're wondering how they reacted to your little stunt at the condo?"

"Yeah, basically. Contrary to what a lot of people seem to think, I don't like making new messes. If trouble is coming, it's more convenient to know in advance so I can deal with it before innocent people are hurt."

"There is no such thing as an innocent person," Vincent insisted. "There are only varying degrees of corruption."

What? Did he and Tahir attend the same cynicism seminar?

"I don't believe that. What about children?"

He laughed. "You went to a fancy magical boarding school."

"Yeah, what about it?" She eyed him a little suspiciously.

Vincent leaned forward and his grin turned vicious. "Come on. I didn't, but I guarantee you there were a bunch of stuck-up assholes there who tried to make your life miserable. Or if not you, other people. It was mostly kids, but the same cruelty was still there, wasn't it?"

Cruelty and dark wizard corruption.

Alison sighed. "I can't honestly say everyone there was a good person, but most people were."

He shook his head. "I can't believe someone who deals with so many criminals and dark wizards is so naïve."

She gestured to the throng on the dance floor. "There are hundreds of people down there, right? Some of them are good, some of them bad. Do all of them deserve to suffer because they've had an occasional selfish thought?" She shook her head. "You don't understand, Vincent. It's because I deal with so much scum that I understand that most people merely want to live their lives and be happy. Those people are innocent, or at least innocent enough."

The informant leaned back and released an exasperated sigh. "I don't understand you, but I suppose I don't need to. I only need you to keep paying me when you need information from me."

Alison smirked. "At least some people are constant."

"It's good to be predictable in business. So, you want to know about the Eastern Union?" He raised an eyebrow.

"Yeah. How have all the different Eastern Union groups in town reacted after what I did?"

"You should never pay in advance." Vincent picked his drink up and swirled it. "You paid too much for the information I'm about to give you."

"It's my money to waste. So, what's the word?"

"Everything's calm," he replied. "Very calm. The specific guys you confronted have been rather open about how you challenged them, but I think you left them confused."

"How so?" Alison frowned, a little confused herself.

"You have to understand that most of the Eastern

Union groups think of you as someone who will kill them if they get too uppity."

"I've let plenty of Eastern Union members go when they weren't stubborn idiots. I always give everyone a chance. I actually give them a few chances."

Vincent shrugged. "Sure, whatever you say. I'm simply telling you what they think, and so everyone—not only the team you attacked—is confused as to why you didn't kill anyone."

"Will I regret it?"

"Who knows? You put the fear of a goddess into them, for sure. The Eastern Union group you helped won't even look for revenge against the others. They have a little truce now."

"I didn't help anyone," Alison insisted. "I rescued a kidnapped woman, someone they shouldn't have involved, to begin with."

He studied her with a hint of incredulity. "That's the big takeaway."

"That I didn't help anyone?"

The informant shook his head. "There's some confusion about why you helped her. No one believes you'd help a random gangster for money. The talk seems to be focused on the possibility that you might be enforcing a 'no kidnapping women' policy on all local groups."

She thought that over for a moment and shrugged. "I won't go out of my way to police the Eastern Union or any other criminal group, but yeah, you can tell people if they ask that I support that policy."

"Here's a little bonus for you, Dark Princess. Do you know that because they believe that, some of the groups have leaked info to the cops about trafficking?" Vincent snickered. "Now I'm sure it's convenient that it often hurts some of their enemies, but the police have already made some big arrests in the last few days. They're merely keeping quiet while they move on the other tips."

Alison glanced over at some twirling, scintillating orbs that rose above the dancers. "Honestly, I won't cry if all the local scum decide it's wrong to prey on women. I don't even care why they are doing it as long as they do it." She smiled as warmth spread through her body. "Consider it my early Christmas present to the city. Now if only the rest of my December can go as well." She stood. "Thanks, Vincent. That's all I needed to know."

He raised his martini. "Have a good night, Dark Princess."

CHAPTER FOUR

Bill's heavy boots thudded against the cold metal floor of the hallway. He approached the reinforced door of the main security office and placed the ID badge connected to his lanyard against the black square beside the door. After a few seconds, the door clicked open, and he pulled the handle.

Four white stations defined the area. A row of stun rods hung on the wall beside several rifles on metal racks. He patted the stun rod hanging from his belt absentmindedly. In the year he had worked for the lab, he had never done anything exciting outside of training exercises.

A drawer containing rifle magazines, both conventional and anti-magic, lay directly in the wall. All the weapons and ammo were stored behind a hardened plastic case secured with a DNA lock. He assumed they only didn't require DNA locks on the main doors because, by the time a typical shift was over, the lab personnel would end up with half the skin on their finger missing.

He squinted because the room was bright—too much so. He always felt like he was in a doctor's office. It didn't help that most of the other personnel walked around in lab coats.

A scoff almost escaped his mouth. The scientists and technicians thought they were too good to mix with the mere security guards. If anything ever happened, the snooty assholes would hide behind the men with guns, yet they still showed no respect.

"Hey, Mark," Bill said cheerfully to the other blue-uniformed security guard present. Even though eight guards worked any given shift, most pairs barely saw each other, meaning Mark would be his only real source of conversation for the next several hours.

The other man sat behind the security monitoring station and typed on his keyboard. Three different monitors were linked to dozens of cameras that covered every corner of the facility. Too bad nothing interesting ever happened on them. He had joked about changing one of them to baseball or Louper with one of the scientists, and the man had spent fifteen minutes lecturing him about security protocols.

Bill moved to his desk and sat. He checked his single computer screen for any security alerts or messages. Everything was as normal as it had been yesterday, the day before, and all the months prior.

He snickered. "You know, when I left the service with my security clearance, I thought, 'Hey, I can get myself a great job.' And here I am, a security guard. No one knows about this place, and no one will break in. Do you know how I know?"

"Yes," Mark replied. "You've whined about this before." He rolled his eyes. "Because there's not enough security."

"Exactly. That means they don't actually care." He shook his head. "Damn. Sorry. I'm simply bored out of my skull today."

Mark grunted with little evidence of sympathy. "You're paid well to be bored. Do what I do. I love pointing out how much money I make without a degree to the dentist I live next door to. He's such a smug prick, but I make more than him. Shit. I think he's still paying off dental school, and he's been practicing for fifteen years." He grinned. "You know what they say. 'Work smarter, not harder.' I busted my ass as a corporate security guard for nothing, and now, I make money sitting around doing nothing but staring at monitors. You say you're bored. I say I'm blessed."

"Yeah. Blessed. Whatever you say, Mark." He stood and made his way to his colleague. "It gets a little boring without being able to bring anything in is all I'm saying." He pointed to one of the monitors. Lab-coated scientists swarmed around a table and blocked the view of the table's occupant. They couldn't see a reflection in the glass wall of the room that might provide even a glimpse of the test subject, whom they had taken to calling the project. That made it easier to deal with.

Mark shrugged. "Maybe we should learn chess or something. I'm sure we could print a set from one of the lab 3D printers."

Bill nodded. "It's more fun than looking at the project. Poor bastard." He winced. "When I first started working here, I had some nightmares about that guy. It's kind of freaky."

His colleague shook his head. "The guy was basically dead when they brought him in. Think of it like organ donation. It's easier to handle that way. If they get this shit working right, it'll save many lives, and all it'll take is some dead people."

"It never bothers you?" He studied the man curiously. "You never think about it what it might mean?"

"I don't get paid enough to think about what it means, and I don't do anything I don't get paid to do or that doesn't get me laid." Mark shrugged. "And they said he was a volunteer."

"Yeah. I'm sure they didn't explain what he was volunteering for." Bill scoffed. "I'm not saying I plan to quit, but the whole thing does freak me out." He made a face. "I wonder who he is. With all the DoD money that flows in here, it's not like they're trying to make the world's best accountant. That means whoever they started out with had to be someone who knew how to fight."

"Sometimes, it's better not to ask too many questions. It's not like knowing the answers will make you feel any better." Mark frowned and narrowed his eyes.

All the cameras in Lab A2 had died, the same location where they currently experimented on the project.

The two security officers exchanged glances, their unease mirrored in each other's faces.

"Should we do something?" Bill asked and swallowed.

Mark shook his head. "We follow protocol. There are four guards in there. It's probably only a glitch. Let me try to restart the feed." He tapped in a few commands, but the cameras remained dead. "Huh. There's been no system interruption, which means there's something wrong with the cameras themselves."

The bright lights of the room dimmed, and red emergency lights kicked in. A loud alarm buzzed.

"Warning, warning," a synthesized female voice announced from the ceiling intercom speaker. "Primary loss of containment noted in a class five laboratory. Full alert warning issued. Protocol alpha is in effect. All security personnel please converge on laboratory alpha two. I repeat, all security guards please converge on laboratory alpha two. Lethal force is authorized."

"What the hell?" Bill shouted. He hopped up and rushed over to the weapons rack. He waved his ID over a black panel and placed his thumb against the small silver DNA sampling square. A faint burning sensation followed, and the case opened. He grabbed a rifle and nodded to Mark.

"It's probably a mistake," his colleague muttered as he stood, but he still walked over to the weapons rack and selected a rifle.

"Mistake? I've worked here for a year, and they've never had anything like that." He shook his head. "Come on. You know the procedures as well as I do. Someone had to activate the full alert." He nodded at the blank displays. "Something has happened. You know what the protocol says. They've sent it up the chain, and now, it's time to do our jobs."

Uncertainty lingered on Mark's face. "Damn it."

Bill stuffed anti-magic magazines into his pockets.

"Damn it? We finally get to do something. We'll go save some of those stuck-up assholes' lives and earn ourselves a sweet Christmas bonus." He slapped a magazine into his rifle with a grin.

The other man continued to mumble while he gathered his ammo and prepped his weapon. "Or they fire us for killing the project and wasting billions of dollars of private and government research funding."

He scoffed. "You heard the recording. Lethal force is authorized. If we don't follow procedures, we can get in trouble. Now, let's go waste ourselves a Frankenstein."

They rushed out of the security office.

"Frankenstein's monster," Mark corrected.

"Huh?"

"Frankenstein was the man who made the monster, not the monster's name." He shrugged.

Bill rolled his eyes. "I don't care. Let's simply kill him and get this over with."

They rushed down the narrow corridors.

"The only thing I don't understand is how the bastard woke up," he muttered after their first turn. "Don't they have some sort of kill switch on him?"

"I thought so," the other guard replied. "It might be that it has nothing to do with him. Maybe something else exploded. It's not only tech, right? It's all that magic. Can't you accidentally summon a genie or a demon or something?"

"I don't think it works like that." Bill frowned, his breathing a little heavy from their run. "But I'm not sure. I tried asking once about what exactly they did, and one of the scientists told me if I asked too many questions, they would fire me."

They sprinted down another hallway. Several turns later, they arrived at Lab A2. The outer door lay on the ground—scorched, by the look of it.

Bill took up a position beside the door. "Okay, not a false alarm."

Mark stopped right behind him. "Three, two, one."

Both men rushed into the lab, their guns at the ready.

Smoke choked the air, which made it difficult to see. Bodies littered the floor—scientists, technicians, and the other security guards. Several were badly burned, almost beyond recognition. Others were less torched, but deep, blackened burns marred their chests or backs. A sea of glass shards scattered between the corpses, remnants of what had once been the glass wall marking the project's "room."

The examination table at the center of the room lay on its side, partially melted. Damaged parts of the electronic equipment smoldered and sparked. Various liquids lay in puddles on the floor, including blood.

"Oh, fuck," Bill muttered. He swallowed and tapped a code into his smartwatch.

Another alarm sounded.

"Project containment breach," the computer announced. "Protocol beta is in effect. Phase I withdrawal order. Facility will now be sealed in ten minutes. All personnel evacuate immediately."

Mark jerked his head toward Bill. "Are you fucking insane? We're not authorized to order escalation without express permission."

"If we're not allowed to do it, they shouldn't have given us the code." He swept the room with his rifle. "Look at this shit. We can't let that bastard get outside." He nodded. "Come on. The protocol doesn't say we have to stay here. Let's go. The project doesn't tour the damn lab. He might have gotten out of here, but he doesn't know the way to the exit."

His colleague stared at one of the dead security guards. "He killed them."

Bill snorted and pointed to the scorched stun rods lying beside them. "They didn't have rifles with anti-magic bullets. Now earn your fucking pay so you can make fun of the dentist."

Both men rushed out of the lab. Screams echoed from down the hallway.

"Damn it. The bastard." Bill sprinted toward the sound and Mark hurried after him.

They turned a corner and found two more dead bodies. A muscular naked man with a shaved head stood over them. Silver-gold implants were embedded throughout his body. Golden arcane glyphs glowed on his forehead, chest, arms, and legs.

The project turned toward them, his solid black eyes unfocused.

Bill raised his weapon. "Look, pal, you need to surrender right now. Mark and me, we always treated you nice, right? Never said shit to you. So why don't we go back to the lab and talk about this? None of this has to be a big deal."

He tilted his head to study the two guards and raised a hand. It crackled with red-orange energy.

"Fuck this. I'm not dying here." Mark gritted his teeth, flipped his safety off, and fired.

The bullet ripped through the target's shoulder, and he jerked back, his mouth twitching.

"The enemies of the United States must be eliminated," the project intoned, his voice a low rasp.

Mark swallowed as the wound in the man's shoulder began to close. "You have to be fucking kidding me. Did you know he could do that?"

Bill shook his head.

"The enemies of the United States must be eliminated," the project repeated.

"Woah, woah," Bill shouted. "We're Americans. This isn't a battlefield. We're not terrorists."

A bolt of energy erupted from the escaped man's hand and struck Mark in the chest. He catapulted backward and the acrid smell of his burnt flesh filled the air as he collapsed.

"Shit. Die for good this time." Bill flipped to burst mode and opened fire.

The project jerked several times but didn't fall. "It hurts," he protested as his flesh began to knit itself together.

"So much for their stupid anti-magic bullets." The guard turned and ran down the hallway, but two thick security doors slammed shut in front of him. "No, no, no!" He spun around. Two other doors closed behind the project. He was now locked in with the revenant killing machine.

"Warning," the computer voice intoned from an intercom. "Phase III withdrawal initiated. Initiating protocol gamma. Facility has now closed. Self-destruct has been activated."

"You sons of bitches," Bill screamed. "You're watching, aren't you? You're watching, and you've left us here to die."

"The enemies of the United States must be eliminated," the project growled and raised his hand. Energy flowed around it as he readied another attack.

Bill threw his rifle to the ground and banged against the security door. "Don't you get it, you zombie freak? The final emergency override has been activated by someone remotely. The big boys know you broke out. You'll never escape." He laughed hysterically. "You'll burn with me. We're both dead. Well, fuck, you were already dead. This time, it'll stick."

The project's head jerked, and his eyes twitched. The vacant look vanished, replaced by cold determination. Awareness. "No. I'm not, and I can't die here." He threw an energy bolt into Bill.

Pain exploded throughout the security guard's chest. The blinding agony killed the scream that wanted to erupt. He fell to his knees and onto his chest, his eyes fixed on the aberration in front of him.

"Y-you won't escape," he wheezed. "You're not a person anymore. You're merely an experiment."

The lights flickered. Bright light poured from the glyphs on the man's body to encase him in a blinding nimbus. Red-orange lines of energy flowed from his hands and wound around him.

"I will escape," the project reiterated and the field of energy around him grew brighter and denser.

"They'll...come for you. You're too...dangerous."

"They'll leave me alone, or I'll make sure there's nothing left." His eyes twitched a few times, and the vacant look returned. "The enemies of the United States must be eliminated."

Bill closed his eyes and let the darkness take him almost in time to avoid the pain of the explosion.

CHAPTER FIVE

The elevator dinged, and Alison stepped into the building's lobby, holding a small box. It contained a few keepsakes from her condo. She wasn't sure why she hadn't brought them to her new place earlier. Most of her things had already been moved, including her furniture and clothes.

Was it some sort of psychological block? Me not wanting to really accept that I moved in with Mason? Ava could have found me a company to pack up my apartment and have it moved within a day, but I insisted on doing it myself. I kept telling myself that made sense, but it really didn't. I'm a busy woman with money.

She sighed and slowed to a stop.

It didn't make sense. Every time she thought about her relationship, she circled to the same truth. She had no problem living with Mason. Everything had gone well since they'd moved in. It'd only been a few weeks, but they'd already stayed over at each other's places before enough that there were no surprises left.

Alison grimaced. She knew what the real problem was. In a recent phone conversation with her dad, he had asked a simple question that changed everything. Had she met his parents?

There was nothing wrong with them from what Mason had told her. They were disappointed when he didn't follow in the family footsteps and become a healer of some sort, but he remained in communication with them. He, though, had met both her parents more than once.

She sighed. Moving in with him marked another step on a path with an ending that made her uneasy, even though she loved him. Meeting his parents would be one more.

What is it about Brownstones and pulling the trigger on commitment? Is it because we're a one and done kind of family?

No. That's not right. The only reason it took so long with Dad was because he obsessed over an epic proposal thanks to what Mom had told him.

Alison blinked. Marriage? No. She couldn't think about that, not yet.

Or does all of this seem inevitable to Mason?

Quick movement out of the corner of her eye caught her attention. She spun toward the source and her heart rate kicked up. Her fingers flexed instinctually as they prepared to drop the box and summon a shield. That level of magic was unnecessary to deal with the middle-aged manager in a suit who smiled at her.

"Oh, hey, Ryan," she stated. "You startled me."

"I didn't mean to sneak up on you." He chuckled. His smile wavered, and he took a deep breath. "Although that's hard lately. I've actually tried to catch you these last few weeks, but you're never here anymore." He sighed. "I know that's what moving is, but you're doing it so slowly, I would have thought I would have seen you more."

"I've still worked a lot of jobs," she explained. "So it's been almost a quick ninja thing. Pop up here, grab a few things, and head on out. I should have hired a moving company, after all. I moved not all that long ago, but I forgot how annoying it can be."

Ryan nodded slowly but his face remained doubtful. "I understand all that, but I won't lie about how sad I am that you're moving. I was convinced I could get you on the condo board. You were the only real celebrity living here. Oh, by the way, you never did tell me where you were moving to."

Alison hadn't wanted to give him any details, but it did seem rude when she thought about it. "I moved in with my boyfriend." She frowned as she thought that through. "Or maybe he moved in with me. I bought a house, and we both moved into it. The logistics were a little complicated, but this is the best solution we came up with."

"A house? How nice. Where is it?" All the sadness vanished from Ryan's face, replaced by warm curiosity.

"It's on Mercer Island. I found a nice five-bedroom, two-story right on Lake Washington," she explained. "There is plenty of room for Mason, me, and Sonya."

"Sonya?" He looked confused for a few seconds before understanding dawned. "Oh, that shy teen girl you're taking care of? That's very generous of you by the way. I only talked to her once, and the only thing I could get out of her was, 'Hey.'" He worked his jaw for a few seconds. "And Mercer Island lakefront property? I haven't checked the prices lately, but unless they've cratered, you need to add at least one extra zero on the price of one of these condos to get in the ballpark of what a halfway decent house there costs."

Yeah. It wasn't only a halfway decent house. Why do you think I ended up buying it instead of Mason?

"It wasn't...cheap. Relatively speaking, but you know, the best home is the best home." Alison shifted the box in her hands and a few of the photo frames inside rattled. "And I decided I wanted something a little more private than a condo. It's better for Sonya, too. She's gone through a lot, and I think having her in a totally different living arrangement will help her relax more."

"That makes sense," he agreed. "And I have a hard time thinking any kid wouldn't enjoy living in a huge lakefront house."

Alison chuckled. "Yeah, that's probably true."

Ryan gasped, and something approaching hope slid over his face. "What are you doing with your condo? Are you selling it? Renting it? I would *love* to rent it." He licked his lips. "It would be weird to sell mine and buy yours, wouldn't it?"

She managed not to grimace. There was being a fanboy, and there was being a creeper. Then again, the man was far more interested in collecting Brownstone memorabilia about her father than her.

It doesn't matter. We're not really neighbors anymore, and I don't need to come over here much.

"I'm not sure," Alison admitted. "I'm still thinking about that. While selling it would make the most sense, there's no urgency to sell, and I don't know if I want to bother with the hassle of selling it at the moment."

"Keep in mind that you can get way higher than normal list price," Ryan insisted. "Being a celebrity and all." He looked abashed. "And here I am thinking I'd be able to afford it."

Alison replied with a shallow nod. It was time to escape and sometimes, the easiest escape was the most direct.

"Sure, thanks. Um, I'm sorry, Ryan, but I'm on the clock." She held the box up. "I'll see you around. I should be back at least once more."

Ryan nodded quickly. "See you around. You can always call me if you need any help or advice."

"I'll keep that in mind." She headed toward the front doors and her mind lingered on the condo's disposition. There was one practical reason not to sell it. If an enemy gained access to the condo, there was the potential they could use the emotional resonance against her in spells, but with enough effort and magic, she could take care of that. Keeping the condo and updating the wards would take far less work in the short term.

Is that why I don't want to sell it? Because it's tedious or because at the back of my mind, this is simply me hedging against Mason?

Damn. I should have been like Sonya. She fit everything she owned in a suitcase.

A long pier stretched from the edge of her property, her own personal jetty into the water. Alison sat in her back yard in a lawn chair and stared out over the lake.

Thick clouds clogged the gray sky. That combined with the chilly wind didn't make for a beautiful day, but there was an eerie beauty to the expanse of calm water.

Huh. I should probably get a boat. But I can fly, so isn't that pointless? Although flying isn't as relaxing as looking at the water. But then again, I don't have to be in a boat to look at the water.

"It's forty degrees out here, A," Mason called from behind her. "Not exactly lounging weather, and I don't sense any magic from you."

She turned to where he stood in a brown jacket, his hands in his pocket and pointed to her jacket. "I have a coat on. It's not like I need magic for everything."

He chuckled. "I'm surprised to see you out here. You've barely been outside since we moved in. I thought it was because the weather sucked, but the only thing decent about today's weather is that it isn't raining."

Alison stood with a smile. "I don't know. It's a good spot to think. Watching the water relaxes me. It's funny. I was never all that into the beach when I was growing up in L.A. I'm a freshwater girl, maybe." She shrugged. "I'm still young enough that I'm learning things about myself. Go figure."

A stiff breeze caressed her face. The jolt of cold fought against fatigue. It was refreshing in its own way, although abrupt.

"What has you thinking so much?" Mason asked.

"Mom."

"What about her?"

"I called her earlier today," Alison explained. "I only wanted to check on her. She told me she doesn't suffer from any morning sickness, even though she had some potions prepared in case she had any problems with it. Now, she jokes about how she scared it away and she wasted the effort of having the potions made."

"After meeting her, I wouldn't be surprised if she did manage to scare it away." Mason grinned. "She can be intense. I don't know who will kill me first if I ever seriously pissed you off—your mom or dad—and I'm not sure which would make it more painful."

Probably Mom. Dad would make it quick, but I don't think I'll mention that.

"Yeah, she can be intense, which makes sense all things considered." Alison blinked a few times. Her lips parted. "A baby's coming. Talk about intense."

Mason gave her an appraising look. "A, what's wrong? I thought you were happy about the baby."

"I am happy about the baby." She sighed. "Life and death. Every time I think about the baby, I think about that. I can't help it."

He nodded. "And you think about Myna?"

"Yeah." Alison pointed toward the water. "I wondered if I should get a boat. It seems so petty to worry about that kind of thing with everything that happened, and it makes me stop and wonder what Myna would have thought about me worrying about it."

"We talked about this. Don't do this to yourself." Mason walked over and placed his hands on her shoulders. His breath came out in visible puffs in the frigid air. "Myna believed in you—the woman you are and your potential in the future. She believed in you more than I think you believe in yourself. While I'm no expert on Oricerans, I do think a woman who was hundreds of years old probably has more insight into life than a couple of twenty-somethings."

She leaned forward to rest her head against his chest and his jacket felt chilly against her cheek. "I know. Mom said something similar. It's not like it's the first time I've lost someone, but it feels like it's my fault. I think that's why I have trouble letting it go. I don't feel guilty about buying the house and worrying about that kind of thing, but I do think a little more about her at times like this."

"It's not your fault. Those dark wizards are the ones who were prepared to flood a city with monsters. Myna helped to save a lot of people." Mason wrapped his arms around Alison. "And there's nothing wrong with remembering the fallen. You simply have to not stay in the past with them. The only thing anyone can change is the future, even someone as powerful as you."

Alison looked up and smiled. "That's what this house is. The future."

"Present and future." He released her and pointed to a low-flying drone headed toward them. "And I think it's a lot better for Sonya than the condo. She seems happier and less stressed here."

Alison waved to the drone in the distance, and it changed direction. "Maybe we should have all moved to a cabin in the woods. If I ever master portal magic, we'll do exactly that." Her smile faltered. "That does make me think."

"About?"

"All the Drow princesses out there," she explained.

"What about them? No one's contacted you since Rasila." He shrugged.

"That doesn't mean they're not coming." Alison extended shadow wings and lifted a few feet. "I might not have as great a technique as all of them with much of my magic, but the power I represent is too tempting. After all that crap a couple of months ago, I'm convinced they won't leave me out of this queen crap." She released her wings and lowered to land in a crouch. "Based on what Rasila said and what Myna told me, they probably won't try to kill me, but that doesn't mean they won't cause trouble."

Mason laughed.

She frowned. "What's so funny?"

"A, we're security contractors. We are paid to deal with trouble. Worry about the problems in front of us and deal with the Drow when and if they come." He nodded toward the house. "But I have a feeling they won't bother you for a while."

She followed him as he headed toward the back door. "True. That gives us more time to set up wards."

Mason chuckled. "If that makes you feel better. Sure. But do me a favor."

"What?"

"Try to not go looking for extra things to worry about." He shook a finger at her. "I'll cure you of that Brownstone gloominess."

Alison rolled her eyes. "I'm not gloomy."

"Says the woman who literally flies around with wings made of shadow." He grinned.

"Very funny."

"Hey, at least you're smiling." He winked. "The pasta should be close to done. That's originally why I came out to get you."

"That sounds great."

Alison closed the door behind her and rubbed her cold hands together. Mason was right, and she had to remind herself of the conversation she'd had with Andrei.

I'm only one woman. There's only so much I can do.

CHAPTER SIX

Hana knelt in front of Omni, a small plate with a carrot beside her. The pet sat on her living room couch and was currently in the form of a small brown rabbit. His nose twitched adorably. He had been in that form for most of the day but had started the morning as a brown kitten.

"You're such a good and special boy," she murmured. "Yes, you are. Mommy loves you." She held a small orange carrot between her fingers. "But if you really want the goods and the love, you have to give Mommy what she wants."

Omni's nose twitched, and he crept forward.

The fox raised her other hand. "Now shake."

Omni raised a paw and placed it in her hand. She squealed in delight, and the rabbit stared at her.

Tahir looked over from the dining room table where he worked on a tablet, his wand slotted into an interface connected to the side. "What's so exciting?"

"You weren't paying attention at all?" she asked.

He shook his head. "I don't find that animal nearly as interesting as you do, but I do appreciate that you enjoy his company, so I endeavor to let you have your time together."

She chuckled. "I don't know if I should call you selfish or thank you for that. But that's not important right now." She nodded at the paw in her hand before she held the carrot out. Omni nibbled on it happily. "See?"

"I see a rabbit eating a carrot," her boyfriend responded. "Which isn't something I find of particular interest, even if the rabbit can change shape."

"No. The carrot's a reward for a new trick, babe." Hana rolled her eyes. "I taught him to shake, and that's on top of the trick I taught him yesterday. It's getting easier." Hana set the carrot on the couch and stood. "He's super-smart— way smarter than some dumb non-transforming pet. It's almost like he understands me."

"I doubt he understands you in the sense you're talking about." Tahir pointed to the eating rabbit. "He's merely associated sounds with actions."

"How is that not understanding what I say?"

"It's conditioning, not language. He might be smart for a beast, but he's not demonstrated true sentience." The infomancer tilted his chin, a haughty look in the eye.

Hana laughed. "Don't be jealous, babe. I love you as much as I love Omni."

"I'm on the same level as the pet. I don't know if I should find that reassuring."

"You should." A satisfying survey of the living room followed in which Hana took in a large bird cage, a terrarium, and multiple pet beds with different textures. Cat and dog toys littered the floor, along with a series of paper and cardboard tubes. Bags of different types of pet food and seeds sat stacked in the corner. Omni seemed to prefer the food expected by whatever his current form was at the time.

Her gaze settled on a large aquarium. They'd purchased it weeks before, but Omni had yet to turn into a fish. Thus far, he'd become several different small mammals, birds, and lizards. All had four limbs, and none of the species appeared to be exotic, but he was always brown in color and roughly around the same size and weight. She wasn't sure if he was still a baby, and thus if he would grow any larger, but he hadn't grown in the weeks since she'd found him.

"You've been so many things, my perfect little trans-forming boy. You make Mommy proud." A long sigh escaped her lips. There was one mild sticking point, a faint disappointment with her otherwise perfect pet.

Tahir set his tablet down. "There are only so many tricks you'll be able to teach him a day. Don't convince yourself that you can make him do whatever you want merely with enough love and effort. He might be an unusual animal, but all indications remain that he is an animal in the end."

Hana shook her head. "It's not that. I'm totally satisfied with his tricks. I'm merely disappointed that I've not seen him transform yet. I thought it was simply luck the first few weeks, but now I wonder if he doesn't change in front of me on purpose."

Tahir frowned a little and curiosity filled his eyes. "That's an interesting observation. I hadn't thought about it, but I've never seen him directly transform either. I've felt it, but I haven't seen it."

Hana bobbed her head. "Exactly. I can smell the magic when it happens, but I want to see it."

"I doubt he's trying to annoy you."

"I get that, but I really want to see it. Does he contort before your eyes? Does a glowing field surround him? It might be cool."

"It could be utterly mundane," he replied with a shrug and folded his arms. "There's no particular reason to imagine it's impressive to witness personally. I'm an info-mancer. My most useful and powerful spells are far less visually flashy than some lackwit thug's fireball."

"Sure, but why don't we ever see it?" She frowned. "There has to be some reason for that, babe. If he doesn't do it on purpose, then what is it?"

"It might be that the magic doesn't work when some-one's looking directly at him," Tahir suggested. "I'm not saying it's a conscious choice, but simply a fundamental aspect of how it works. I also wonder if we should resume looking more into his background. There are a number of questions lingering about him, as your statements prove."

Hana stroked the still eating rabbit's fur and scowled. "If we ask around too much, it might turn out King Oricer-an's his owner and wants him back. We ask around, and the next thing you know, an army of Light Elves shows up outside and demands His Royal Furryness back." She scoffed. "I don't want to give up my awesome pet to King Oriceran. He's already king of a planet. Why does he need Omni? That selfish son of a bitch."

"Calm down, Hana." The infomancer laughed. "Before

you work yourself up into launching a single-handed attack against King Oriceran. Keep in mind, we have absolutely no reason to suspect that Omni belongs to the king or even an Oriceran."

"Doesn't he have to be Oriceran if he changes shape?"

Tahir shook his head. "Not necessarily. To me, what is significant is that he's changed shapes many times, but every form he assumes is a terrestrial animal."

"I hadn't thought of that."

He nodded. "It's not as if he's sampled the local animals either. Even if his coloring is off, several of his bird forms are clearly tropical in nature, as are some of his lizard forms."

The fox nodded. "True, true. But that doesn't mean he's not the king's." She harrumphed, still angry at the idea of the greedy monarch taking her pet from her.

"I suspect if he had misplaced a pet, he would be able to track him without too much effort." He chuckled.

She sniffed at the air. "Maybe. I'm not so sure."

"Maybe?"

Hana nodded. "It's something I noticed before, but I thought was merely a bonus. His scent is very mild. Haven't you noticed?"

"I didn't pay it much mind."

"Anyway, even when I shift into fox form to try to get him to copy me, I've noticed how mild his scent is. It's like permanent scent stealth. It's not one hundred percent, but if he was out in the woods, I could see how if he changed a few times, it'd be hard to follow his scent and not be distracted by other animals." She shrugged. "A kind of anti-tracking."

Tahir frowned. "Really? I wonder how far that extends." He reached over to grab his wand out of the interface, raised it, and murmured a quick incantation. His frown deepened. "Interesting."

Hana sniffed at the air and a faint sweet smell filled her nostrils. "What are you doing?"

"Checking on your theory. I attempted to cast a tracking spell on Omni." He set his wand on the table, stood, and walked over to the couch where Omni was finishing the last of his carrot. "But it didn't work."

"It didn't work?" Hana tilted her head, confused. "At all? His stealth smell is still there, only reduced."

The infomancer shook his head. "It didn't work at all."

The rabbit hopped off the couch and over to one of his corner cushions.

"What does that mean?" she asked.

"That this creature might be inherently immune to magical tracking," he explained. "It can change shape, has a reduced scent trail, and can't be easily tracked. That's an interesting set of characteristics."

"It's cool, but it's not like it's weird." The fox shrugged. "It probably helped him survive in the wild. There are many weird monsters on Oriceran. If you're small, shape-changing and not smelling are a great way to escape them."

Tahir rubbed his chin. "Perhaps, but it also might be he's not the product of natural magical influence." He gestured toward the rabbit. "It may be that he was created by someone, whether an Oriceran or an Earth witch or wizard. He might be an experiment."

Hana shuddered. "Don't call my precious little Omni that. He's not an experiment. He's simply a cool pet."

"We don't know that. I really do think we should look into him more. The truth is always important, and everything we learn about Omni only raises new questions. I'm not saying he's dangerous, but I am saying we should continue to explore those questions until we find the answers that confirm things one way or the other."

"The truth?" She scoffed. "Screw the truth. I care about having a totally adorable pet who is super-fun and easy to train, babe. I don't even know if I sat down and asked someone to make me a pet if I would have thought of one as cool as Omni." She grinned. "And you haven't even seen the best trick I taught him."

He blinked, a little taken aback. "You're more concerned about showing me more tricks than figuring him out?"

She eyed him with suspicion. "Can you guarantee that learning more about him will help him learn more tricks?"

"No, I can't guarantee that. How could I?"

"Then who cares. Anyway, back to the trick. I saved it to show everyone at work but might as well show you now. Maybe once you see this awesomeness, you'll stop trying to give him back to King Oriceran."

"I'm not trying to give him to anyone," Tahir insisted, his tone exasperated.

Hana's grin faded. She meant everything she'd said about her pet but messing with Tahir to put him off his game might also push him away from some boring investigation.

She clapped and pointed to the couch. "Omni, parkour."

The bunny bounded toward the couch at high speed as if chased by a predator, leapt toward a cushion, and shoved off, his ears twitching. He landed and rolled onto his side, his gaze fixed on her.

The rabbit righted himself and cocked his head at her for a few seconds before he sauntered over to his cushion.

She clapped her hands and cheered. "Good boy. What a smart, good, and fast boy."

Tahir raised an eyebrow. "Very amusing. I'm dubious of the utility of that particular trick, but I can't deny the amusement factor."

Hana rolled her eyes. "Tricks don't have to be useful, babe. They only have to be neat. I'm not training him for jobs. He's my little baby." She sat on the couch and crossed her legs. "I thought of something, though. If he doesn't change when someone's looking at him, that means he won't randomly change on a walk outside, right?"

Tahir nodded. "That would be a reasonable conclusion given the evidence currently available to us. We might be incorrect about our theory."

"Do you think we are?"

He shook his head. "No, I believe we at least have the high-level details correct."

"Then we don't have to hide him anymore." She nodded with a satisfied look. "I can take him for walks in the neighborhood. I can take him to work. I can take him to the dog park on days he's a dog." She gestured toward a litter box in the corner. "If he wasn't using that, I would have been forced to take him on walks."

They hadn't even had to train Omni to use the litter box. They brought one home, and he immediately used it and continued to do so regardless of form. Fortunately, his small size made that aspect of care easy to handle, especially for a nine-tailed fox with a sensitive nose. Tahir had insisted that she deal with the more unpleasant aspects of the pet care, but she didn't mind because it wasn't like Omni snuggled her boyfriend all the time. He was missing out on the best parts of owning a pet, too.

Hana stared at the rabbit and released a contented sigh. "And even if he does change on a walk, it's not a big deal."

"It's not?"

"I think we were being too paranoid before."

"How so?" Tahir asked.

She nodded, satisfied with her thought process. "This isn't Yakima. This is Seattle. We have magicals and magic all around. Alison fought the Fremont Troll and flies through town with shadow wings. I don't think anyone will notice one little magic pet, especially one as small as Omni, even if he's the most adorable thing to ever exist."

"Perhaps." Curiosity spread over Tahir's face. "I do wonder if there's a way to capture him changing, though. Perhaps we should revisit our discussion of internal cameras in the house. I know you don't like them, so I've not set them up, but we should consider it."

"If you want to see me naked, babe, you only have to ask." The fox smirked.

He snorted. "The cameras are for Omni only."

Hana rolled her eyes. "You waste some of my best jokes. I never can be sure if you actually miss the point or are messing with me." She looked at Omni, who had snuggled up on his cushion and closed his eyes. "Sometimes, the best part about a mystery is not knowing the answer. The truth isn't always fun."

"Fun isn't important." Tahir stared at her with a

disgusted look. "One should always strive toward the truth. Giving up on learning the answer is an admission of failure of intellect."

"Oh, babe, I'll loosen you up yet." She grinned. "And I think Omni will reveal the truth when the time is right."

"He's not some creature of a Seer's prophecy," the info-mancer responded.

"You don't know that. Maybe he is."

He scrubbed a hand on his face. "Fine. I'll take what you said into consideration." A little frustrated, he headed back to the table and sat, shaking his head.

Don't worry, my little cutie shapeshifter, Hana thought. *I accept you for what you are. Truth? It's overrated and often boring.*

CHAPTER SEVEN

The general tossed the tablet on the desk in front of him. "This is what happens when you rely too much on private contractors. I understand that we needed the help of the private scientists for development, but I have said from the damned beginning that security should have been all military. Too few guys and shit procedures." He glared at the tablet. "And now we have a big mess to clean up, one of the worst of my career."

The high-level PDA official seated across from him nodded. "It was felt that farming out some of the development in a private-controlled facility would lower the risk of exposure, especially given some of the questions that might arise if the oversight committee became aware of the project. It was also easier to monitor the smaller number of personnel involved to ensure they didn't leak any information about the project."

"It was felt?" the general echoed with a grimace. "It was easier? Think about how you phrased that. It denies any sort of personal responsibility. Of course, that's how we always do this shit. We act like what we decided didn't lead to a fuckup, but it did. Billions of dollars wasted, and an entire facility destroyed. Thirty people already dead." He shook his head. "That's bad enough, but the damned test subject escaped. So much for the self-destruct failsafe." He frowned. "And the story's holding?"

The PDA official nodded. "An unfortunate industrial accident in a remote lab. The few people sniffing around have actually praised the company for locating the lab far from any major population centers."

"Good." The general pointed to graphs displayed on his tablet. "And the test subject's already demonstrating every tax dollar we invested in him." He grunted. "When you came to me with this project, I believed in it. I championed it to some very skeptical people because I thought it could help bolster our national defense. I helped push funding in the DoD budget to get those dollars to Project Revenant. All in all, I cashed in many chips and pissed off more people than I'd care to count."

"And I'm very grateful," his companion replied. "No one could have anticipated the magnitude of the containment failure. We're still going through the data, but somehow, he was able to disable or overload the anti-magic emitters set up in the walls of the lab. It shouldn't have been a problem when they examined him."

He scoffed. "No one could have anticipated. It shouldn't have been a problem. You started as a field agent, right?"

The man nodded. "I joined a few years after the gates started opening and worked my way up. We had more of a caseload in the beginning. The bounty hunters didn't soak up as much of the trouble."

"Then I don't understand how you could be such a fucking moron about this," he uttered bluntly. "You sound like some idiot before the launch of the Titanic."

"Let's keep calm. Insults aren't helpful in this situation."

"This *is* me calm. The point is, I relied on your assurances that the test subject would be contained, and now, he's on the loose. It's inevitable that Congress will come sniffing around, and at that time, I'll have to fall on my sword for this fucking debacle. That notwithstanding, however, we still have to handle the problem at hand."

The general swiped on the tablet to reveal a satellite map of Washington state. "This is why I wanted this shit done on some island. The only smart thing these idiots did was stick that lab in the middle of nowhere, but there are still too many towns around, and if he hits the highway and goes north or south, he could easily get to Portland or Seattle."

"At that point, containment is assured." The PDA official shrugged. "The test subject is powerful, but the resources of a major city, even non-military, could handle him."

"Assuming he doesn't kill hundreds of people first. You're PDA. You've seen what a high-level magical threat can do in the middle of a city." The general slammed his fist on the desk. "The point of Project Revenant is to protect Americans, not endanger them. We need him contained before he gets anywhere. All the people who died at that facility were buried under enough NDAs and security clearances that even if someone asks, we can deflect without having to explain ourselves. If he shows up and wastes a group of people in some pissant town, we won't be able to cover that up. Congress will want to know what happened. The President will want to know what happened. Are you willing to go to the President and say, 'It was said, sir…'"

The other man gritted his teeth. "We're already both in agreement that destruction of the test subject is necessary. Project Revenant is a failure, and it's time to cut our losses."

"Fine." He drew a deep breath. "And how do we intend to clean this up? If I push for military assets, it'll ring too many bells, and people will ask what the hell is going on. And I'm not so fond of the idea of risking men and women in uniform to cover up our mistake. I have a feeling whoever we send after the test subject will lose at least some of their people."

His companion shook his head. "Our private partners are still laboring under the impression that should they handle this matter successfully, they might be able to restart the project. They have private resources they maintain for this kind of situation."

The general frowned. "What? More security guards?"

"No, highly trained personnel accustomed to highly dangerous magical enemies. The assets deployed are unaware of the nature of the target." The PDA official smiled. "As far as they're concerned, he's a high-level terrorist bounty who escaped from an ultramax and subsequently destroyed the lab while looking for weapons. They'll handle him, and even if they suffer some losses, we won't have to explain it away."

"You're confident in this?" He raised an eyebrow. "And I don't want to hear any shit about 'It is said' or other deflection. I want to hear you say you believe this will work."

"I know this will work," the man replied. "I'm familiar with some of the personnel used. They've helped with certain other messes in the past."

The general stared at him. "Project Revenant isn't your first spin at the wheel, huh?"

"We both have our secrets, General, but everything I do, I do for the protection of our country."

He nodded. "Then let's hope your friends can protect the country from the monster we already made to protect our country."

Alison linked her fingers and stretched her arms above her head. She stood near a wall in the tactical training room along with Hana, Mason, and Drysi. "I'm sure it's very impressive, Hana."

The fox shook her head and regarded her friend with faint disappointment. "It's pet parkour. You're damned right it's impressive. I can't believe you don't think it's as cool as I do."

I have to be careful. It's like saying something bad about Omni is like telling Hana her kid sucks.

Mason finished casting his shield, strength, and speed spells before he slid his wand into its holster. "I'm not so sure we should bring that animal here."

Hana groaned. "You're as bad as Tahir."

The life wizard laughed. "I don't know if I should be insulted or happy."

"I don't really want Omni here," Alison confirmed. She raised a hand at Hana's dirty look. "Not because I think he's dangerous, but because I don't want to establish a policy of people bringing their pets here other than the fish in the tank. It's honestly not a good idea. We could be attacked at any moment, and for all I know, people might be allergic to him."

The other woman's shoulders slumped. "That makes sense." Her eyes turned vulpine, and her glowing tails appeared as her nails grew into claws. She raised her head, irritation on her face. "But now, I have a fair amount of anger to work out." She nodded toward the *tachi* resting against the side of the wall. "I'll go all claws today."

"Your choice." Her boss shrugged.

Drysi removed her jacket and tossed it near the wall. She wore a custom tactical vest filled with knife holsters. "I won't lie, even though I've worked here for a couple of months, I still can't get over how posh even your training is." She gestured to the maze of tunnels and ramps that filled the room.

"I learned the importance of team training from my dad," Alison replied. "We've done well, but I still feel we haven't fully gelled as a team. Vancouver proved we could kick major ass together when we need to, but I want to continue these twice-a-week major sessions for a while." She looked around at her friends.

No one seemed annoyed. Hana's face reflected eager anticipation. Drysi and Mason both wore excited expressions.

Okay. I'm not pushing them too hard. If I were, they would tell me. There is nothing wrong with having them train a lot. Dad had the OGs train even more than this, but not all of them had the kind of experience my people do.

Drysi cracked her knuckles. "Being on a team is stranger than working in your posh simulator room. I'm used to people saying, 'Oy, it's that bloody bitch coming for us, but at least she doesn't have any friends.' I'll admit I never believed I needed backup for a tidy job until I met you."

Alison smiled. The Welsh witch had adjusted well to Brownstone Security over the last couple of months. Although she hid behind humor, she mixed freely with other employees and no one had much bad to say about her, even if they had admitted they were still cautious about her, given her background.

All these things take time, but I started this company with a former criminal, and as long as Drysi is always looking forward and not backward, I'll have a place for her.

Alison pulled her phone out and tapped in a few commands. "I've initiated the program. It'll start in two minutes." She set the device on the ground. "It's a simple exercise today—a horde battle. They'll generate randomly. Ava said there will be a portal."

The witch eyed her and some of the mirth faded. "So... what? We try to kill them all?"

She nodded. "Sometimes, we bust into penthouses and stun people, and sometimes, we nuke every monster in sight. Fun times."

Mason and Hana both nodded as their expressions turned grim.

Do they see through this? Do they know I want to make sure I don't have to depend on some combination like my dad and Myna if we ever run into another problem like that jar in Vancouver?

Alison jogged up a ramp, but no one said anything else. They fell in behind her and waited in silence as the seconds ticked away. She took a deep breath before she summoned a shield and a shadow blade.

"Everyone, form up," she ordered. "We won't know where the initial attacks will come from."

They all adjusted position so they had total visual coverage of the room.

Drysi drew a dagger. It glowed red as she licked her lips. "Waiting's always the worst part."

Hana crouched and nodded.

Mason inhaled deeply and pulled his wand out again.

A shriek echoed around the room. They spun toward the source, and a swirling simulated portal appeared. Giant bat-like creatures with razor-sharp claws emerged from the gateway in a steady stream, two or three at a time.

"This is what I get for telling Ava to surprise us." Alison summoned shadow wings and launched upward. "Okay, let's do this." She flung a shadow crescent with her free hand to slice a bat in half. It disappeared in a flash.

The system didn't have to make the bodies disappear, but it was hard to maintain a large number of bodies and the active simulations. Even technomagic had its limits.

The stream of new arrivals broke into three separate lines, now. The loud cries of the creatures echoed and overlapped to produce a distracting cacophony.

Drysi threw two daggers into the swarm. The explosion blew several of the enemy out of the air and they disappeared before they hit the ground.

Mason released fireballs into the moving group and burning creatures cried out before they disappeared.

Despite the efficiency of the Brownstone team in destroying the simulated monsters, more emerged from the portal every few seconds.

Alison flew back and a few yards higher. "I'll see if I can overwhelm the portal. Cover me." She raised her hands and channeled magic into a growing orb.

Several bat creatures swept low in an attack on Mason, Drysi, and Hana. The nine-tailed fox bounded forward to tear into one with a claw before she vaulted onto another to rip into it from above. It disappeared and dropped her onto a third, which she finished off quickly in a flurry of claws.

Okay, that move wouldn't work in a real fight since our enemies don't tend to simply vanish, but I can't complain about her results.

Mason concentrated his suppression fire on the creatures swarming Alison. Drysi tossed an explosive dagger every few seconds, and it was enough to keep the enemy from overwhelming them.

Alison waited for a hole in the swarm and released her channeled energy. The blue-white orb sailed across the room and struck the portal, exploded, and incinerated a handful of the nearby monsters. The portal vanished, and several other creatures flickered and vanished as well.

"Crap," she muttered. "I think I damaged some of the emitters again." She summoned a shadow blade and sliced another attacking monster in half. "Ava gave me a real earful last time about that. It's apparently really difficult to source some of the components."

Drysi whirled and flung a dagger into a dense cluster of

the enemy. The resulting explosion obliterated four with one strike and she yelped in triumph.

Hana thrust up and ripped the throat out of a monster. She dragged herself up and jumped off the creature's body in one fluid motion before it disappeared and repeated the same attack until she ran out of victims and corpses and stairs.

"Hana!" Alison shouted. She dove toward her friend, but too many enemies blocked her path.

The fox plummeted. She caught the edge of a wall with her hand and hauled herself over it onto a platform.

"That was fun," she shouted with a huge grin. "Hot Fox Bat Parkour. Now, how's that for an awesome trick?"

"That was bloody brilliant," Drysi shouted before she hurled her last dagger. The attack annihilated several more enemies.

Alison conjured another shadow blade and carved through the monsters around her. Mason had holstered his wand and now picked off low-flying attackers with punches that landed with loud crunches. She turned, ready to slice through more creatures.

Hana ripped into the last bat with both sets of claws and a merry grin on her face. The simulated enemy vanished, and she shook out her claws.

She's enjoying that a little too much.

Alison blew a breath out as she glided down to the platform and released her blades. "That went even better than I thought it would." She frowned at Hana. "I know it's training but be careful. I don't want you to develop bad habits."

The fox waved a hand dismissively. "It's fine. I have this

all under control. Besides, you saw it. You have to admit it was damned cool."

Mason smiled and nodded. Drysi grinned.

Her boss folded her arms and took a deep breath. She smiled. "Yeah, it was damned cool."

CHAPTER EIGHT

Hana burst into Alison's office a few hours later, her eyes wide and her breath ragged. Alison blinked and looked up from her computer and her stomach knotted. Had something happened to Sonya?

"Did you run here?" Alison asked.

The other girl nodded quickly. "I thought about foxing out, but I didn't want to freak the rest of the staff out."

She took a couple of deep breaths. "What's going on?"

The fox all but leapt into the seat in front of the desk. "I've had an idea. A stunning idea. A brilliant idea. Perhaps my best idea today."

"Your best idea today?" She didn't hide the confusion and incredulity in her voice. "Okay. Let's hear it. I'm willing to discuss something if it's not ridiculously expensive or dangerous."

"Dancing." Hana spread her hands apart in front of her face. She opened her mouth in a smile and tilted her head, her eyes wide. Something about the expression came off more insane than happy.

"What about dancing?" She frowned. "Somewhere between the start of this conversation and now I got lost in Siberia."

"It's simple." Her friend smiled. "Let's go dancing. It's been a while. You haven't wanted to go since… You haven't wanted to go in a while." She maintained her happy expression even though her voice wavered near the end.

Yeah, I haven't wanted to go since Myna died. And I guess you're right. Mason would say she would want me to move on. She would say I should move on, but it's hard for me to do that.

I need to constantly remind myself I have to live for both myself and Myna now. She might have been an ancient Drow warrior, but she was also the kind of woman who appreciated a good bowl of noodles. She enjoyed life, and I should, too. It's one way to honor her sacrifice.

Alison took a deep breath and nodded. "Okay, you're right. It's been a while. I wouldn't mind a little dancing." She made a face. "But not at the True Portal."

Hana snickered. "You're not still bitter about the Halicans acting like you weren't hot enough, are you?"

"No, it has nothing to do with that. I don't want to mix work and pleasure. Does that make sense?"

"I don't care, to be honest. I never liked the vibe at the True Portal anyway." She clapped. "This will be great. Sienna already agreed. I asked her before I ran down here."

"Why did you run down here?" Alison asked. "It isn't like this is something vital you had to ask me about within seconds. You also could have sent me a text."

"It was a great idea, and I wanted to share it with you." Hana shrugged, and her expression suggested she didn't understand why her friend didn't understand the importance of sprinting to her office to coordinate evening plans. "And why text when you can talk?"

Drysi stepped in front of the open door on her way to another destination.

Hana leapt up and spun toward her. "Drysi!"

The witch jumped back, and her hand jerked for her wand. She blinked several times and took deep breaths. "Bloody hell, woman. Don't do that. You're lucky I didn't have a bloody dagger on me."

Alison shook her head and chuckled.

The fox chuckled sheepishly. "Sorry. I wasn't trying to freak you out. You simply happened to be there." She pointed at Alison, herself, and Drysi. "Her, me, you, and dancing. And Sienna. You like Sienna, right? I've seen you talking to her before."

"I don't have anything against her." The witch's face pinched in confusion. "I've chatted with her a few times. And dancing? As in for fun? Or is this some kind of job? I don't do dresses, to be clear."

"Then wear jeans and a T-Shirt. I don't care. If they don't want to let you in, I'll charm them." Hana winked. She stuck her hands on her hips and offered the other woman a look of disbelief. "And this isn't about a job. I know Ava could probably kill us all with her pinkie, but most of the administrative staff aren't the kind of people who can pick up a rifle and gun down a half-dozen guys. Why would I bring Sienna along on a job?"

"How do I bloody know what you would do?" Drysi lowered her hand. It had lingered near her wand while irritation lingered on her face.

She jokes with us all the time and acts relaxed, but she's still a woman who spent years as a bounty hunter and dark wizard assassin. It'll take a long time before she doesn't see someone trying to kill her around every corner. The fact that she trusts us as much as she does is almost a miracle.

"Come on," the fox whined, her palms together in front of her. "It'll be fun. It's all low pressure. Since Alison and I already have guys, we only go to have fun. But if you find someone and want to go off with him, we've totally got your back, too." She stuck her lip out. "And if you don't come, I'll bitch at you until you do. The Hot Fox Overwhelming Whine Attack. Ask Tahir how well it works."

"I don't know." Drysi glanced at her boss with uncertainty on her face.

Alison smiled in response. "I do think it'd be fun, but I won't whine at you if you don't want to come."

The witch shrugged. "All right. I suppose it couldn't hurt."

Bodies packed the dance floor, but unlike at the True Portal, the club was almost entirely human with only a few elves scattered through the crowd. Infectious energy and joy radiated from the pleasure-seekers. The entire club was exactly what Alison needed, an affirmation of life.

Dancing, cooking, Mason. Friends. I let a life sneak up on me this last year. Too bad I can't convince Izzie to move here. I think she'd love it, but she has more baggage than even Drysi to work out. Still, she did mention looking into dating, of all things. So who knows?

She smiled as she continued to survey the dancing

throng, her ears protected by a silence spell that surrounded her table. She'd already danced many songs with her friends, but she wanted to be able to have a conversation without shouting. Drysi sat at the table with her, but Hana was still on the floor, her body one with the beat and a carefree look on her face.

The Welsh witch gulped beer from a bottle. As she'd stated earlier, unlike Alison and Hana, she didn't do dresses. Her jeans and shirt, though, were far tighter than she normally wore, which enabled any potential admirers to appreciate her lean, athletic frame.

Alison hadn't pushed her on any guys, even though Hana had tried. Drysi needed time to find herself. That much was obvious.

"Too bad Sienna had to pull out," Alison commented. "She's fun to hang out with, but I wouldn't want to go dancing either if my mom was in the hospital. Thankfully, it sounds like everything will be all right."

Her companion nodded, a curious glint in her eye. She brushed her bangs from her face. "I'm surprised, but maybe it's only because I still think like a member of the order. It'll be a long time before I don't. I hate myself for thinking like that, but it's the way it is."

"What do you mean?" She watched the other woman carefully. She trusted Drysi, but in a lot of ways, she was still getting to know the real woman and not the fake image the witch had originally presented to earn her trust.

"I'm surprised you would socialize so much with a non-magical." The witch shook her head and shrugged. "Don't get me wrong. I'm not trying to tell you I think you're wrong, but I won't lie and pretend I feel as comfortable about the equality of magicals and non-magicals as you do. I'm getting there, and if I have to spend the rest of my life being the opposite of Conrad, so be it. Eventually, I'll be more like you and less like him." She frowned at her beer. "I'm a bloody great friend to bring on a girl's night, aren't I?"

"Being yourself is good enough for me, and you're my friend, and I'm glad you're here with us." Alison considered the woman's words for a few more seconds before she added, "I grew up not knowing I was a magical. I'd like to say that's the reason, but Hana doesn't have a problem with non-magicals and neither does Mason." She gestured to the back of a skinny man dancing a few yards away. "The dark wizards want to think of themselves as better than everyone, but I don't know if that's something they can really do in our world anymore, especially with technology."

"They let themselves forget what they were supposed to be—or maybe it's that they never were that." Drysi sighed. "It's hard to realize everything you believed in was bullshit."

"Not everything. In the end, you wanted to honor your family." Alison offered a comforting smile. "And you can do that going forward."

Hana bounded away from the edge of the densely packed floor and wiped the sweat off her forehead. She adjusted her short red bandage dress before she sat at the table with her friends. "Why did you leave early?" She nodded at Alison. "I know you only left because she left."

"I hate that song," the witch explained.

"I love that song. The beat is ridiculous." The fox shuddered with a smile on her face.

"It beat the UK's entry in Eurovision the year it came out. I lost a lot of money betting on the UK that year. It taught me never to bet on Eurovision, but it also left me bitter toward that bloody song."

Hana laughed. "Fair enough." She leaned closer to Drysi. "That guy you danced with earlier is still eyeing you, and he wasn't the only one." She pointed to the witch's blue-streaked hair. "This helps you stand out. You should get out there and work it more."

"I'm not done. I needed a little drink." She raised her bottle with a smile. "It's been a while since I let go."

The fox smirked and eyed Alison. "It reminds me of a certain Dark Princess when I first met her."

Alison picked her glass of water up and took a sip. "So you are having fun?" she asked Drysi. "I know we badgered you into this, but I want you to have a good time. We can always do something else if you don't like it."

Hana stuck her lip out to pout but didn't say anything.

The witch took another gulp of her beer and sighed. "I am having fun, but it's strange."

"Strange?" The fox tilted her head. "What's strange about it? I saw you moving out there. This isn't the first time you've been dancing. You were smiling and having a good time."

Drysi set her bottle down. Her cheeks had reddened in the last few minutes. "No, but it's been a long time since I did something social that wasn't part of a trick or a plan. Relaxing? Having fun?" She shook her head. "I always had a job or a mission. I had to serve the great cause." She shook her head. "And friends? It feels weird dancing with friends because I'm such a right bloody bitch." She snorted and looked at Alison. "I can't even think like a good person. Some days, I wake surprised you didn't slit my throat when you had the chance. I still don't understand what you see in me half the time."

"Don't be like that." Hana rolled her eyes and patted her shoulder. "Alison believes in you, and I do, too. If Mason thought you were a threat to Alison, he would have dumped your body in the bay a long time ago."

The witch snorted. "He's a good man. Keep that one. But that doesn't change the fact I betrayed Alison."

Hana scoffed. "Whatever. When I met her, I was ready to turn her over Eastern Union to save my own ass."

"I planned to assassinate her."

Alison snickered. "I don't know if I like this 'Who was planning to screw over Alison more?' contest. Let's say you're both winners and move on."

The other two women exchanged glances before they burst out in raucous laughter.

She waited for the amusement to die down and pointed to Hana. "You had your reasons, and if you remember, you stopped yourself before you tried anything really stupid. And, Drysi, you've proven yourself over and over again, not only with the Seventh Order but in jobs over the last two months. You have your history, but you don't have to be defined by your past."

"What is it about you, Alison?" Drysi asked and shook her head. "You don't have to show mercy. You're strong enough that it doesn't matter. You could rule through fear."

"It's because I'm strong that I should show mercy." She shook her head. "But tonight's not about mercy or strength or dark wizards. It's about having a good time at the club."

She stood. "Let's all get back out there together and stop moping about a past we can't change."

The witch finished her beer and stood. Hana pushed to her feet and clapped.

The trio pushed into the edge of the crowd. Without the silence spell, the thumping bass and loud notes of the dance music swept over Alison. She raised her arms in the air and half-closed her eyes as she moved with the music. Her friends stayed close, huge smiles on their faces.

It's good to spend time with Mason, but sometimes, it's good to get away. It's been a decent December, and I wonder if I can get through New Year without some dangerous showdown.

Alison spun to Hana's squeal of delight.

Everything will be all right.

CHAPTER NINE

Alison finished toweling her hair and slipped into a soft white robe. Of all the charms of her new home, she was surprised how a small difference in water pressure could make such a big improvement. Magic could be helpful, but the interface of magic and technology, even with something like plumbing, could be more difficult if a person wasn't careful. There was a reason, after all, that even elves on Oriceran didn't use a spell for every little thing.

I never knew what I was missing.

"Yes," Mason commented from outside the bathroom. "I understand. Yes, I get that, too. I'm not an idiot. I thought you of all people would understand."

Alison cracked open the door, confused as to who Mason was talking to. He sat on the edge of their bed, his phone in hand and his brow furrowed. Tension lined his face, and when he wasn't speaking, he gritted his teeth.

"I'm not promising you anything," Mason muttered. "Let's make that damned clear. I'll talk to Alison about it, but it's her company." He snorted. "Yes, she's that, too. I'll let you know soon enough." He sighed and tossed his phone on the bed before he rubbed his temples. "She's always so smug."

Alison stepped into the bedroom and closed the bathroom door behind her. "What's going on? Keep in mind, if it doesn't involve dark wizards or Drow assassination attempts, I don't know how worried I am about it."

"That's our new baseline?" he asked.

"I figure those are more reasonable than 'Don't worry if it's not a Mountain Strider.'"

"True enough." He closed his eyes. "I received a call from someone I used to know. We've talked relatively recently for job stuff, but..." He opened his eyes. "I didn't expect her to call me directly."

"That's all rather mysterious." Alison folded her arms. "Would you care to be a little more specific? I thought we were way past the stage of you thinking you need to protect me without my input. I make the call about the risks I'm willing to take."

"It's not that."

"Who is it then?"

Mason took a deep breath and released it slowly. "Raven."

She bounced the name around in her head for a few seconds. "That witch you had to deal with a while back?" She frowned. "What about her? I didn't press you about her because you said she annoyed you. Now, I wish I had."

"There's something you don't know. She's not merely someone I used to know. I dated her, and it was fairly serious for a while."

"Okay, I wish you had me told before, though." She nodded slowly and lowered her arms. "I'm a big girl. You don't have to hide your exes. I know you've dated more people than me. It's not something I hold against you, especially since my dating life was messed up by my weird issues stemming from school."

He shook his head. "It's not that. It's just…" He chuckled. "I think, honestly, this is more about me protecting myself than you."

"What do you mean?" Alison walked toward the bed. "You don't sound like you're still in love with her."

"I don't know if I was ever in love with her, not in the way I am with you."

She resisted a snort. "Smooth, Mason. Very smooth."

He shrugged. "It's true."

"Then what's the deal with her?"

"The whole situation makes me look like an idiot, despite what I just got done saying to her." He grimaced. "Do you know why I broke up with her?"

Alison shook her head. "I didn't even know you were dating her until right now, and I don't know enough about her or the relationship to even venture a guess."

Mason fell silent for a moment before he took another deep breath. "Raven's different, even for a magical. She has always been dangerous."

She shrugged. "There are many people who would say I'm dangerous, including most members of the Eastern Union and dark wizards."

"It's not like that. There's a core of light to you. There always has been. You have that even though you've had to deal with so much. Most people who went through what you went through as a kid would come out twisted."

"Dad and Mom saved me," she replied softly. "They're the reason I'm good today."

He shook his head. "Be real, A. I'm not saying they aren't good people, but I've met them both, and if they are this intense now, I can only imagine what they were like when you met them. They provided stability, but you were a good person before."

Alison looked away. She didn't want to argue with him about James and Shay, even if she felt he didn't understand how special they had always been.

Mason sighed. "The point is, A, you're a good person. Anyone who deals with you for any length of time figures that out, but Raven always had a dark soul—an edge—from the very beginning when I first met her. I think that's why I was attracted to her, but she went too far. Damn it. She might have been going too far from the beginning, but I refused to see it. I didn't want to face the obvious truth."

"Too far?" she asked. "How?"

"She specialized in potions, but she always wanted to push them farther, to make them more powerful. She resented what she called the 'timidity' of other potion witches. She used to talk about how people can't explore the limits of power if they're afraid of a few mistakes along the way." He scowled. "She decided she needed more dark magic to fuel her efforts and began to take more risks. The potions she made weren't merely dangerous, and many of them hurt the people who used them."

He shook his head. "Raven justified all her experiments by saying she never forced a potion on anyone, but she preyed on desperate people, both magicals and non-magicals, and told them what they wanted to hear. People came to her, whether it was to feel better or because they thought she could make them better, and when people ended up hurt or broken, she claimed it wasn't her fault. Everyone has the right to choose, she always said. She also didn't care—she was always obsessed with the present being more important than the future."

Alison grimaced. "That's twisted."

"Exactly."

"But how did she get away with it?"

"She used her connections and kept a low profile. The people who benefited from her magic did a lot to shield her, and I'm reasonably certain she'd bribed the cops or someone in the PDA either with mind-altering potions or money. I honestly never knew for sure." A bitter frown settled over his face. "I didn't want to be a part of it, but I thought I loved her, so I gave her an ultimatum. One I thought was easy if she cared. Me or that kind of magic, and she chose that evil. So, I left her. Every once in a while, work pushed me toward her, and every time I've seen her, she's only sunk deeper into that crap."

"I'm sorry," Alison murmured.

"There's nothing to be sorry about. I'll say what she always said. She made a choice, and I made my choice." Mason shook his head. "She'd always been fucked up, and now, I feel like an idiot for being with her for as long as I was. I should have seen what she was from the beginning and stayed well clear. She's not like you, A. She's never been a good person. If you still had your soul-sight, I'm sure you would be disgusted by what you saw in hers."

She sat beside Mason on the bed, a thoughtful look on her face. "The way you describe it, she's half mad scientist and half magical drug dealer."

He scoffed. "Basically. I suppose someone could make an argument that she has influence that she wields to keep certain groups from spreading, but that's a thin line to hang any respect for her on." He looked at his girlfriend. "I want to be clear about earlier. It wasn't a personal call. She wasn't trying to get back with me."

Alison arched an eyebrow. "But she's tried in the past?"

"Yes, but I've made my position clear, and she knows I'm with you." He managed a grin. "And even if she wasn't totally twisted, she'll have to try much harder if she wants to convince me she's better than the Dark Princess."

She laughed. "It's nice to have a reputation that scares your boyfriend into staying with you." Her smile disappeared. "But if it's not personal, what's it about? I heard enough to think she wasn't asking you to be a bodyguard."

"Before we go into that, I wanted to make sure you're okay."

"Why wouldn't I be okay?"

Mason shrugged. "You've taken all this well. I feel bad about not being more honest about my past before."

"What? Did you want me to throw you across the room in a fit of jealousy?" She smirked. "I'm not that petty."

He chuckled. "No, but I do know how you like to hold things in, and I know I have to prod you to get you to rely on me sometimes."

"I trust you," she replied. "If I didn't trust you, I wouldn't have moved in with you, and some crazy ex from your past won't change that."

"Fair enough."

"So what does Raven want?"

"She heard about how you helped an Eastern Union member," Mason explained. "It's convinced her you might help her, and she wants to hire Brownstone Security for a job."

Alison frowned. "What job?"

"Raven didn't say, but she did imply that you would have an interest in helping her even without payment." He shrugged apologetically. "She says she can't involve anyone else because it's too dangerous."

"Too dangerous for her?"

"Probably. Even if she's a hundred percent honest and everything she's doing will help other people, there's no way this doesn't end with her not benefiting the most."

She sighed and rubbed her temples. "The older I get, the more I appreciate the wisdom of my dad trying to keep things simple by focusing on paying bounty jobs. Between this and Andrei, I feel like I'm being swept up in every random thing that happens in the Seattle underworld."

"I don't know if your dad's any better," he pointed out with a chuckle.

"Huh?" She blinked. "What do you mean?"

Mason gestured with his hand. "What about that thing in Denver? It wasn't only one guy he took down."

"Technically, at least some of the people involved had bounties. Uh…" She shrugged. "And that was barbecue-related. Things are different for him when it comes to barbecue. I think Dad would invade a country if they threatened barbecue. But let's focus on your crazy ex-girl-friend and what she might be up to."

"She wasn't so much crazy as evil," he corrected.

Alison gave him a stern look. "And that makes it so much better?"

"No, it doesn't, which is why I dumped her, A, remember?"

"I'm messing with you." She lay back on the bed and stared at her ceiling. It could use a new coat of paint. Millions of dollars, and it still needed improvements. "And I trust your judgment. Do you think this might be some kind of trap? I'm not interested enough in Raven to purposefully walk into it unless you think it might be useful."

He shook his head. "That's not Raven's style, not really, especially against someone she knows is powerful. She's not the kind of witch who likes to get her hands dirty, and she's a coward. She's survived as long as she has by trying to develop mutually beneficial relationships with powerful people, not screw them over." A hint of steel underpinned his words.

"Again, I have to say this really makes me question your taste in women." She sat up. "And it doesn't sound like you think this is a good idea."

"I don't know. It's hard for me to separate my professional judgment from personal feelings in this case, A. It's like I said, Raven won't do anything that doesn't benefit her, so even if this ends up helping other people out, she'll come out on top."

"I can live with that if it means fewer innocent people will suffer in the long run." Alison shrugged. "It's at least worth checking things out. She might be evil, but she might also be worried about something or someone eviler than she is."

"The enemy of my enemy is my friend?"

She shook her head. "Not necessarily, but we can at least hear what she has to say."

Mason nodded. "Sure, but we shouldn't meet her on her own turf."

"I thought you said you don't think it's a trap."

"I don't, but I also want to put her off her game and I don't want her to think she can take any opportunity to try anything even remotely questionable. The less comfortable she is, the more chance we have to control the situation, and if it ends up being something we're interested in, we can maybe help but limit how much she gets out of it."

"Should we say we want to meet at our building?" she asked.

He shook his head. "There's no way she'll agree to that. She's too paranoid."

Alison considered other possibilities for a moment before she responded with a quick nod. "I have an idea for neutral ground, but I think you should be the one to invite her. That way, she stays under the impression that she has the upper hand."

Mason frowned. "Why would she think that?"

"Because everything you've told me about this woman convinces me that she's arrogant enough to believe you still want her—if not openly, then on some subconscious level." She stretched and headed to her dresser to get a nightgown. "If she wanted to hire me directly, she could have called the company directly, like Andrei. Instead, she chose to call you because she thinks she can still manipulate you."

"I don't feel anything for her, A," he insisted.

She opened the dresser and fished out a nightgown before she turned toward Mason with a soft smile. "I didn't say you did. I'm saying that she thinks you do, and I'm fine with that. We can use it, and it doesn't hurt to meet with her. If we don't like what she has to say, we can always leave. At this point, I'm more curious than anything. She has a reason for wanting me to help, and it's not only to get at you. So, let's see what your evil and crazy ex has in store."

"Evil and crazy now? The list grows."

CHAPTER TEN

"Vincent looks kind of pissed," Mason whispered into Alison's ear as they reached the familiar landing at the True Portal.

"Yeah, he keeps looking from me to Raven," Alison murmured in response. "I think he doesn't like the fact that I've shown up to talk to her here without having come to him first."

A red-cheeked dwarf in a rumpled suit wandered past them and wobbled slightly. A heavy stench of liquor surrounded him.

How the hell did he get so drunk already? This place just opened.

She forced her attention away from the descending dwarf and to their reason for coming.

Raven sat in a corner. The lithe, olive-skinned woman wore a black dress so tight that Alison almost thought it was painted on at first. A gold ring glinted in her nose. She sipped from a glowing blue drink as she watched them and the corners of her mouth turned up in an amused smirk.

Wow. I just met her, and I already want to punch her in the face. This isn't jealousy, though. She simply has an annoying air about her—and again, I really have to question Mason's taste.

He stopped, put his hand on her shoulder, and leaned in closer. "I know Vincent's here a lot, but what are the chances he would be in here right after opening when you happen to be meeting with Raven? Someone told him you would be here."

Alison nodded. "It doesn't change anything. The minute we agreed to meet her in public, we knew it would get out that I talked to her or helped her. She nodded toward the table. "Let's get this over with."

The couple made their way to the table and passed through a silence barrier a yard out from the seating. They both sat after offering the other woman curt nods in greeting.

Raven set her drink down and ran her finger along the rim. "Oh, Mason. It's so good to see you again in the flesh." Her gaze drifted to Alison. "And the Dark Princess. An honor, really. You might not believe that, but it's true."

Alison waved off an approaching waitress. "I won't complain about someone saying nice things about me, but I also won't insult you by lying to you."

The witch raised a delicate eyebrow. "Oh? What would you have to lie about?"

"The fact that I'm happy to meet you." Alison raised a hand. "And it's not about you dating Mason. It's about why he had to leave you."

Raven chuckled and ran her tongue over her bottom teeth. "Did he feed you a story about what an awful and immoral woman I am?" She smirked. "He used to like it when I was immoral with him."

She stared at her with a tight smile.

Do you think that's all it takes to rile me up?

"Watch it, Raven," Mason snapped. "If you want our help, you'd better not piss us off."

"Don't be so sensitive." The woman sighed. "He always was too uptight. It makes sense he ended up with a woman like you, Dark Princess."

"You don't even know me," Alison replied coolly.

"Don't I? The adopted daughter of the Granite Ghost. The dark wizard hunter. The hero of Seattle." A hint of sarcastic mockery crept into her tone. "The underworld fears you, and even the government brings you on to help them out when things get out of hand. I know exactly what and who you are."

She shrugged. "There's nothing wrong with people showing respect for my skills."

"You can't make a better world. You think you can because you're powerful, but you're not all-powerful. You'll learn that someday and stop being such a child."

"I'll take that under consideration," she replied easily.

I don't know if I should be pissed that she's insulting me or happy that she's not trying to convince me to become Queen of the Underworld.

Raven picked her drink up and took a sip, her gaze locked on Alison the entire time. "You know it. You've seen it. Both worlds are broken. They always will be. Such is the twisted nature of all living things, and even gnomes die in the end. The only thing we can do is take some small pleasure during our time."

Mason grunted but didn't say anything.

Alison rolled her eyes. "I'm not some kid who has never seen the world. Your edgy nihilism doesn't impress me, Raven."

"Nor should it." She set her glass down. "I will say this, Dark Princess. You're not the first woman Mason's been with since his mistake in leaving me, but you're the first I don't feel completely contemptuous of."

"Gee, thanks. I don't know what to say."

His nostrils flared. "We're not here for your bullshit, Raven. We're here because you wanted to hire the company, so give us a reason not to leave."

Raven clucked her tongue. "So impatient. Fine. I'll stop having my fun. The job is simple. I need an armed courier service staffed by people with impeccable morals and a lack of greed, along with extreme power and willingness to use it in defense of themselves."

Alison frowned. "We're a security company, not a courier service."

"True, but you do tick all the boxes I need better than anyone probably in the entire Pacific Northwest." She picked her glass up and gulped the contents before she set it down and wiped her mouth. Her hand shook slightly for a second and she lowered it beneath the table. "You're my first choice. Not my only choice, but my preferred choice by far."

Mason nodded when Alison glanced at him.

"What's the package? And you'd better not say it's a person."

Raven laughed. "Of course not. It's what I'm known for. It's a potion."

"You need us to transport a potion?" Alison furrowed her brow, feeling more confused than annoyed at this point. "And you can't use even a high-value courier and lie about what it is?"

The witch shook her head. "This is a...bad potion. A very bad potion."

"And what does that mean, exactly? From what I've heard, you specialize in bad potions."

"Then what I'm about to tell you should convince you even more to help me." Raven fell silent, and her lips parted. She looked aside for a moment before she refocused on Alison. "The potion is being sent to a specialist friend of mine, another potions witch who specializes in the disposal of dangerous magic.?

"What the hell have you done, Raven?" Mason asked.

"What I have always done," she replied, pride in her voice. "Push the limits, but even I understand that some things I do might push the end of tomorrow closer for some."

"And you suddenly care about other people?" Alison asked.

Raven laughed. "I care about myself, Dark Princess. Hurting large numbers of people brings the authorities and angry royals...like you. I understand my presence is tolerated because I know how far to push, and all my clients come to me." A wistful smile appeared. "I give people what they want, no more, no less, but this potion..." She shook her head. "It's dangerous. It was meant to be an experiment in pain, a curse combined with poison, but it won't confine itself to one victim. Such a thing is useless to me but too dangerous to leave around. I thought about hiding it and fleeing Seattle, but I do wish to come back here someday."

"So you're saying you're leaving anyway?"

The witch nodded. "This potion was made at the behest of a business associate. This man and his group are interested in having the potion for their own uses—none of them good, I'm sure. They haven't come after me directly, only because I had the foresight to set up a conditional curse before I went into business with the man. He has a few months left before he can try to kill me directly. I'll have my fun and come back then. Either it will be time, or I'll survive."

Mason folded his arms and snorted. "And who is this business partner?"

"Alphonse Tatum."

The bodyguard grimaced. "I thought you were smarter than that, Raven."

Alison frowned and looked from one to the other. "Who is Alphonse Tatum?"

"I'm not surprised you haven't heard of him before. The guy's a snake, but he's very, very good at keeping a low profile." Mason shook his head. "I mostly know of him from local life wizard circles. He's like Raven. He's interested in how magic can be used to modify people, but he's far more interested in the future, rather than fun times in the present. I didn't know he was back in Seattle. Last I heard, he left town a few years back because the government was looking into him."

Raven sighed. "He's such a dreary man, but he has access to excellent resources. He came back a few months ago and approached me. He had certain rare ingredients I hadn't been able to work with. From what he told me, he'd spent time traveling, most recently Texas, but had decided to return to his home. I'll admit some failure of judgment in this matter."

Alison snorted. "Why should we help you dig out of your problem with this asshole?"

"I'm not asking you to do that." The witch smiled thinly. "I'll leave and either kill him when he comes for me or the opposite would happen. I don't have a basis to convince you, I believe, to protect me from such a man and nor would I want to owe you for doing so. But presuming I survive, I'd like to come back to a Seattle that doesn't regard me as a dangerous terrorist, which is what might happen if that potion isn't properly disposed of and Tatum gets his hands on it."

"If he comes after it and we eliminate any of his men, he'll assume we're defending you, too." She narrowed her eyes. "You're trying to rent a shield for a ship."

Mason scoffed. "That's why Vincent's here, isn't it? You leaked the meeting. You wanted everyone to know you were meeting with Alison."

"So many accusations," Raven responded with a smug smile. "But let me remind you that you chose this location. I would have been happy to meet you at my premises."

"And that's why you're not going to the PDA? From what you've said, it sounds like you've made some sort of magical chemical weapon. Shouldn't they handle it?"

The witch shrugged. "I considered it, but let me ask you this, Dark Princess. Do you trust the government completely?"

"They won't want something that dangerous around," Alison countered.

Raven sneered. "Everyone has heard about how there was a dark wizard plant in the PDA. Even if you trust them or other government agencies here in Seattle, do you trust them everywhere? Do you trust them to dispose of a potential weapon they might study? Right now, I guarantee you that someone, somewhere in the vast bureaucracy of the government is doing an experiment with magic that they shouldn't—one that will probably hurt people—but you'll never hear about it because they'll clean up after themselves." The smug smile returned. "I can't be the only one who forgot about their Broken Wand in L.A. It might have been years ago, but their mistakes almost destroyed a city."

Alison took several deep breaths. Part of her wanted to blurt the truth about what had happened in Los Angeles with her father, but that was one secret the woman didn't need to know.

"You're not a genius, Raven. You haven't made something they haven't made themselves."

"No, I'm not a genius, Dark Princess, but I did have access to the Tears of Eternal Lament." Her smile transformed into a knowing grin.

"You're lying." Alison flinched as if struck. "There's no way you had some of those."

Mason frowned and looked from one woman to the other. "What are the Tears of Eternal Lament?"

"A legendary potion ingredient," she explained. "Some out-of-control gnome alchemist was the one who allegedly made the original batch thousands of years ago. No one has ever been able to replicate what he's done, but small amounts of his material have survived and are ridiculously valuable, even by Oriceran standards." She shook her head. "I used to think it was total crap, only a story, but when I was on Oriceran, several of the older Drow confirmed it was true. There was even a big incident a thousand years back in Drow territory because someone made a summoning potion with a Tears sample. It ended about as well as you'd expect."

"Okay, so it's some powerful potion ingredient, but what does it do, exactly? I don't get it."

"Potentially everything," Raven murmured, an almost euphoric look on her face. "It's pure, concentrated power. A kemana in a drop. Some claim the gnome is from a kingdom that no longer exists, that his sacrifice for the original batch of Tears was that kingdom. Others claim thousands of victims or the hearts of all he loved most dearly, but the details don't matter. All tales point to tremendous sacrifice. That's why they are the Tears of Eternal Lament. They allow potions to accomplish things that otherwise wouldn't be possible even with the careful preparation of magic."

"And you used that because you wanted to make some perfect pain potion?" He shook his head and his face scrunched in disgust. "You're even more fucked up than I thought."

"The Tears have transformed it from a mere potion to something that can spread," she clarified softly. "My ambition exceeded my ability, and now, I'm asking you to handle this matter—not to save my life, even though that might be a side effect, but because even I think some things shouldn't exist. The power of the Tears is now dispersed, but I doubt that will stop the government from wanting to keep the potion for research."

Alison took a deep breath. "Fine." She stood and took a few steps to stare at the other woman. "Before we proceed, I'll check for any artifacts. I need to make sure you don't have a truthbender on you."

"I'd prefer that Mason check me." Raven fluttered her eyelashes.

"Yeah, I bet you would. Now, let's do this. I'm thinking about helping you against my better judgment and because I want to make sure this crap is destroyed, but don't make me regret it, or it won't only be Alphonse looking for you."

The witch stood and spread her arms to the side. "Do your worst. I might still enjoy it."

A few minutes later, she had confirmed the lack of a truth-bender and the truth of everything else with a spell. That left a few details to clear up.

"It's a simple enough job," Raven explained and licked her lips. "I already have the potion secured in a warded containment box. All you have to do is take it to my contact, a witch in Richland. She specializes in the disposal of dangerous materials. She even has a nice day job and helps the government clean up the Hanford Nuclear Reservation."

Alison nodded. "And are there any other special restrictions? Does it blow up if you fly too high with it?"

The witch looked confused. "No, nothing like that. It

shouldn't be a problem. As long as you don't open the potion, there shouldn't be an issue."

"Then you have got yourself a courier company."

Mason glared at the witch. "You said you were leaving?"

"Yes," she responded. "Once I know the Dark Princess has the package, I'll depart for an extended period."

"It's probably best if you never come back," he stated coldly.

Raven laughed quietly, the mockery clear on her face. "Better for whom?" She stood. "Don't worry, Mason. I won't trouble you for a while."

CHAPTER ELEVEN

Alison lingered in the entrance to the parking garage. Mason would be down in a few minutes, and they would drive together to collect the potion. From there, they planned to transport it to Brownstone Security and take the helicopter the rest of the way to Richland, which would take them to the southeast corner of the state.

She hadn't been sure about using the helicopter, but in the end, had decided Mason and Drysi had enough magical power between them to shield the vehicle if it went down, and she herself could ensure the potion made it to the ground safely.

This is my life now, preparing for my helicopter to be shot down, but if I have a few minutes, I might as well take care of things that don't involve people trying to kill me, maybe only people trying to kill my boyfriend.

Alison pulled her phone out and dialed. The unusually dry December had pushed her mind away from Christmas, but a comment by Hana about Christmas presents for

Omni after their briefing shoved the upcoming holiday into the forefront of her thoughts.

"Hey, Alison," Shay answered. "I didn't expect a call from you again so soon."

"I wanted to check on a few things. Christmas is coming up in a few weeks." She chuckled. "Not that you'd know it up here. It's the same old gray Seattle and no snow. They say we probably won't get any until January."

"It goes decades between snow in L.A., Alison," Shay replied. "So I think you're closer to a classic Christmas than we are."

"Anyway, I wanted to iron plans out. Are you cool with Mason and I coming down for Christmas? We discussed it a while back, but I wasn't sure."

"Of course we are. Were you worried we wouldn't be?" Her mother sounded confused.

She laughed. "I can never be sure with Dad. The last time I talked to him about Mason, he seemed fine, but maybe he was filled with brisket and wasn't thinking straight."

"I don't think it works that way unless he's added some very strange ingredients to his sauces." Shay snickered. "Your dad really likes Mason, which is saying a lot. If you want to come, we'll be happy. If you don't, we understand that, too."

"No, I want to come, Mom, especially since you're pregnant. I also thought about bringing Sonya, but she wants to stay here, so she'll spend time with Tahir and Hana. I think if it wasn't for Tahir always stuck in teacher mode, she might prefer to live with them, even with the less space, but I'm happy to let her stay with me."

Thomas barked over the line.

"Quiet, dog, I'm talking to Alison," the woman muttered. She cleared her throat. "I'll need to see your new home. It looks damned fancy from the pictures."

"It's nice, yeah."

"You achieved my dream." She laughed.

Alison shifted the phone slightly. "What do you mean?"

"I originally wanted to live on an island, remember?"

"It's not a tropical island, Mom," she replied.

"An elite island filled with rich people? That's close enough."

Mason stepped through the door and nodded to her.

She nodded back. "Okay, Mom. I have to go. I'll talk to you in a few days. Love you."

"We love you, too, Alison, and you're always welcome here."

She waved to her boyfriend and headed toward an SUV. There was no way she would risk her Fiat.

An expanse of green and brown extended below Alison and she leaned back in the helicopter seat. Patches of white scattered below. Not everywhere had been as snow-free as Seattle.

Glyphs covered the sides of a narrow, dark box that rested in her lap. Raven had shown her the contents before sealing it—a vial filled with an unassuming clear liquid. Not everything dangerous always looked that way.

Is this my month to work for questionable clients? What's next? Some dictator will call me and tell me he accidentally summoned a bunch of rabisu he needs me to put down before they eat everyone?

Alison was tempted to let the PDA know about Raven once the job was done, but the witch was leaving anyway.

At least Andrei has turned away from crime. I have a feeling Raven will wiggle out of this, but I won't let her mistake threaten innocent people. If she comes back, I think we'll need to have a little chat about her career path.

Her gaze dipped to the box. The Tears of Eternal Lament were an evil ingredient, to begin with, but if the witch had at least used them in something helpful, she might have been able to push aside some of her disgust.

So much power and she wastes it.

She glanced at Mason. He was relaxed with an easy smile, the helicopter controls in his hands. Although they flew on air dates every once in a while, he hadn't had nearly as much time in the helicopter lately. He never complained, but she knew how much he enjoyed it. Her boyfriend might be a wizard, but there was still a little boy inside him who was excited to be able to fly an expensive toy.

She adjusted the mic on her noise-canceling headphones. It was impossible to hear anyone unless they shouted over the rhythmic thump of the blades. They could use the receivers, but they'd found they picked up too much background noise the last few times they'd tried.

"Tahir, Sonya, how we doing?" Alison asked.

"No unusual air traffic reported, and I don't see anything with the drone I have following you," Tahir responded. "I've monitored Raven's place, and I've not seen any sign of Tatum, assuming he hasn't changed his appearance."

"Yeah, I'm only watching around the helicopter still," Sonya added. "But I haven't seen anything. This is the world's most boring sight-seeing tour so far. It's as bad as the time Jerry's team guarded the stupid tour bus. Stupid, boring rock stars."

Alison smirked.

Most teen girls would have been excited about that job.

She peered out the side of the aircraft. A snow-capped peak stood off to the right—St. Helens, a sleeping sentinel waiting to wake again and vomit out its ancient anger. The clouds had remained sparse since they'd cleared the city and now granted her a clear view of the wounded mountain.

"Boring sightseeing tour?" she echoed. "You're not impressed by the volcano? Even if you don't care that it's a volcano, it's a pretty mountain."

The team had decided to not fly directly from Seattle to Richland. A small detour for a visual tour of Mt. St. Helens didn't seem like it would be too much trouble, and Alison hadn't really had a good view of the mountain before. They mostly tended to stick close to Seattle when they used the helicopter.

"I grew up in Washington," Sonya replied. "They went on and on about that stupid volcano all the time in school. It was so lame. Blah, blah, St. Helens erupted with the force of hundreds of atomic bombs, even the mightiest wizards would be hard pressed to match it, blah, blah." The girl scoffed. "Boring. Who cares?"

Drysi snickered from the back of the helicopter. "Volcanoes are boring? And I thought I was jaded."

"Yeah. Boring." The teenager sniffed disdainfully.

Hana sat beside Drysi in the back. "Sonya's right. When you grow up here, you hear about the eruption all the time. If it's not that one, then it's all like, 'Oh, no, any day now, Mt. Rainer will erupt and make St. Helens look like a fart.'"

Alison snickered. "I get that. Growing up in L.A., no one thinks about the fact we have earthquakes, but I remember seeing tourists all but wet themselves in a restaurant once when a very minor quake happened, while I simply ate my soup."

Mason glanced at her with a smirk on his face.

"It was very good soup, and there are a decent number of earthquakes in Washington."

"What kind of soup?" he asked.

"French Onion." She shrugged.

"There is one interesting thing about the mountain," Hana commented with a vulpine smile. "I've heard rumors that St. Helens isn't natural. That it was some sort of creature or a mound surrounding a giant monster, one that would make the Fremont Troll look like a gerbil."

Tahir scoffed over the link. He was snug in his chair in the Brownstone Security Building last time Alison had seen him.

"Everyone thinks that every natural disaster that happened before the opening of the gates was some magical conspiracy," he commented. "There are still many natural occurrences in the world. Not everything is a hidden monster, gate, or strange bend in reality. Perhaps humanity was too incredulous before but heading into the opposite extreme isn't any more useful."

Mason banked the helicopter slightly to provide a better view of the mountain for Alison, she assumed.

He's so thoughtful. I had planned to ask him to anyway.

"It's not impossible," he suggested, his tone amused. "There was technically a conspiracy to cover magic up for thousands of years. It does make you wonder, and if there was some ridiculous mega-monster in the mountain, it's not like they would advertise the fact if they have no way to control it."

Alison grimaced. "I don't even want to think about what might be hiding in a volcano. The Mountain Strider was bad enough, and something that has the power of hundreds of atomic weapons would be something that even our whole Vancouver team couldn't win against."

"I would like to see the bloody beast living in there." Drysi grinned. "It'd be like something out of an old legend. Don't you want to be legendary, Alison?"

"No, I'm fine being me." She chuckled. "Legends can be strange things. Nereid Island, for example." She glanced over her shoulder at the witch, curious whether the mention of the turning point in her life would bother the woman.

She continued to smile, however, apparently unruffled.

That's good to know.

"My dad and mom have been involved in some really crazy things," Alison continued. "But let's wait a few hundred years until we're all living on Mars before we release anything that might be inside the volcano. I'd hate to see Seattle nuked because some mega-monster rampaged through the bay."

Everyone chuckled.

Hana sighed and rested her head against the back of her seat. "Speaking of strange creatures, we've had those cameras up for a while now, and Omni still hasn't changed on camera. He's been a parrot for days. He's learned a lot of words in this form, but I want to see him change."

"My theory," Tahir interjected, "is that the mere potential for observation nullifies his ability to transform. I doubt he refuses to do it. I wonder if he simply can't even if he wanted to."

"What if some clever bastard used a spell to peer back in time and looked at him?" Drysi asked.

"A good question. Perhaps no one's attempted to look back into our place from the future, or perhaps they're incapable of doing a spell that might actually affect the past given Omni's potential nature. These are the limits of true time magic. I'll admit I've not studied much of that, but what little I've seen is…troublesome. Still, I'm not that concerned considering how few magicals wield such magic."

Alison frowned a little as she thought it over. The Fixer was the only magical she personally knew who could cast that kind magic. The Drow didn't seem to have any real skill with it, but whether that was because they couldn't do it or simply didn't care about it remained unclear.

Sonya chuckled. "You should shut the cameras off for a while so he's not being watched."

"But I *want* to see him change," Hana whined.

"While I understand that, the cameras currently are off,"

Tahir commented. "It's the only way to verify our theory. In fact, let's check on him now." A faint clacking sound passed through the receiver before we spoke again, "Indeed. Omni is no longer a parrot."

Hana's breath caught. "What is he? And is it totally adorable, or is he another lizard?" She made a pained expression.

"Hmm," Tahir began. "He seems to be a ferret. Whether he is adorable is a subjective judgment. Knowing you, I'm confident you would find him adorable."

"Take some pictures," Hana demanded. "We should catalog all this stuff."

Alison laughed. "And you guys haven't checked around at all? You could head down to a kemana and ask. Maybe the Portland one."

"And have King Oriceran's Omni-napping goons show up?" the fox demanded indignantly. "No thank you. Commoners deserve cool adorable friends, too. I'm part of the revolution. And if I have to tear an army of elves apart to save my pet, I'll do it. Don't tempt me." She nodded at the *tachi* lying on the floor in its sheath.

The infomancer had previously explained her strange theory about the source of her pet. Alison had only noted wryly that stranger things had happened to almost all of them, even if she had her doubts about Omni's royal pedigree.

Mason laughed. "Calm down there, Hana. I haven't seen any royal Light Elf guardsmen sniffing around you yet. You don't have to start a war over your parrot-dog-lizard."

"Just saying." Hana harrumphed. "You don't understand the glories of all pets in one, you sad, broken man."

He laughed even harder.

"Let's try to keep the company from having to take King Oriceran on at least for a few months," Alison suggested with a playful laugh. "We'll need to train first, but it wouldn't hurt to ask around about Omni. That's all I'm saying."

"I disagree, and I refuse. Besides, it's like I told Tahir. Not knowing is fun."

"Well, at least he's small, and it looks like he'll stay small. Unlike a dragon."

She returned to looking at the mountain, which now fell into the distance. It was a fun respite in a dangerous mission.

Let's hope we can drop this damned potion off without too much trouble.

CHAPTER TWELVE

The helicopter kicked up dust and rocks as it descended to a helipad at the edge of the modest airport. Mason had been in communication with air traffic control in the final descent, and they didn't have any issues. A flight was scheduled for takeoff in thirty minutes—the tiny white jet visible in the distance—and another plane would be landing in about twenty minutes.

We made it. No angry flying Drow or fighters or dragons. It was a fairly leisurely flight, more like an aerial tour of Washington than a job.

Alison glanced at the glyph-covered box. Most aerial tours didn't include dangerous magical potions.

Mason and I should do this alone when we're not on a job.

A gray-haired woman in a white suit waited, a briefcase in hand, about twenty yards away from the helipad. She held a silver scepter in the other hand.

That's a fancy wand. It reminds me of the time Mom had to go after the Scepter of Dagobert. It'll take me a long time before I catch up to half the weirdness she's run into on tomb raids.

117

The woman raised her briefcase to shield herself from some of the aerial debris.

Alison peered intently at her. She matched the description of their contact, Cassandra, but they would need to confirm it. It didn't require difficult magic to assume another person's appearance, after all, even if it was something she rarely had use for.

According to Raven, the woman would be able to speak a code phrase that would open the box without effort as proof of her identity. Otherwise, they were to contact the witch again for additional instructions and hope they didn't get into a bloody fight at an airport.

The witch had better not have decided to stick me with this stupid doomsday potion at the last minute and flee.

Alison ran the possibilities through her mind. Contacting Latherby at the PDA made the most sense, but she couldn't deny that Raven was probably right. Some temptations were better off not offered.

A light thud sounded as the helicopter touched down and jolted her out of her thoughts. There was nothing she could do now but hope the woman they were about to meet could do what the witch claimed.

She exhaled a sigh of relief. "I was really worried they would shoot this thing down. I'm not that rich that I can afford to lose helicopters. It's also why I've held off on a dropship."

"At least you don't act like I'm going to crash." Mason grinned and flipped several switches to power the aircraft down. "Ladies and gentlemen, welcome to Richland, Washington," he joked. "If there was a flight attendant, she would tell you to get yourselves out of your seats and out of the helicopter."

Drysi and Hana snickered.

"Raven was a little unclear on how long this would take," Alison began as she removed her headphones. She set the box down carefully and opened her door. "But I won't leave until I confirm that damned potion is taken care of. I already feel dirty working for Raven, and I only agreed because of how dangerous this thing is. The last thing I want to do is have to come back here in a few days because Cassandra poisoned the Columbia River."

The others nodded.

The fox grabbed the sword belt. "I haven't been out to the Tri-Cities in forever."

"Tri-Cities?" Drysi wrinkled her brow in confusion.

"Richland, Kennewick, and Pasco," she explained. "I used to know this shifter who moved from Seattle to here. It's...not my thing, but it's all right. There's a surprisingly decent kemana under here. I don't know if it has anything to do with the fact that they used to make nuclear weapon stuff here or not."

The witch grimaced. "Nuclear weapons?"

"They stopped that a long time ago." Hana sighed. "But, uh, they're still cleaning stuff up. I heard there wasn't only nuclear contamination here, though. Rumor is that some of the reputation it had before was the government spreading stories to cover up some of the magical contamination they had to clean up from screwed-up experiments that they weren't supposed to run anyway."

Alison nodded before she stepped out. "Raven

mentioned something about Cassandra helping with clean up."

Despite Mason's early warnings against looking too deeply into conspiracy theories, the truth was the government still covered up a number of mistakes from the past. Knowing about the reality of magic wasn't the same thing as knowing about every terrible plan that some ambitious man or woman launched in the shadows.

Earth was a big place, and groups like the Silver Griffins couldn't stop every rogue magical plot before the gates started opening.

Everyone took a moment to disembark and prepare their defense spells or artifacts, including Hana who used her now preferred choice of a crystal ring. A red glow suffused her skin. There was no reason to let Cassandra take them by surprise if she was a fraud.

The suited woman waited, an impatient look on her face as she watched them.

The Brownstone Security Team formed a triangle around Alison as she summoned her own layers of shields. Decent levels of magic hung in the air and not all from the suited woman, but it was hard to discern the other sources. It could be everything from Alphonse Tatum hiding with a spell to a gnome mechanic deciding to add a touch of magic in a hangar.

The suited woman approached with a frown. With her white hair up in a bun, it was like someone's grandmother coming to scold them. High levels of magic radiated from the briefcase.

"Do you have the item?" she asked and nodded toward the box. "That looks like it to me."

"You're Cassandra?" Alison replied with a question.

The woman nodded once and raised the scepter. "Yes, I am."

Hana dropped her hand to the hilt of her sword. Mason watched the witch closely but didn't move. Drysi held a wide, ready stance and her hand drifted inside her jacket to one of her daggers.

Cassandra arched an eyebrow. "You're all rather touchy. I'm surprised, given what I heard."

"We don't normally do this kind of thing," Alison explained. "And we're very interested in making sure this particular package is taken care of. You'll need to prove who you are before we hand anything over."

"This is why I prefer couriers versus mercenaries."

She frowned. "We're not mercenaries. We're security contractors."

The witch snorted. "Let's worry about trivial differences later. For now, hold the box up. I can prove who I am easily enough."

Alison nodded and complied with the instruction, and her heart thumped harder. The next few seconds would determine whether a fight broke out or not.

Cassandra muttered an Enochian phrase and the glyphs on the box glowed brightly.

"You'll find that you can remove the lid easily now," she explained.

She took hold of the lid and tried to lift it. When it responded easily, she let it drop again. "How long will the disposal process take?"

"About ten minutes." The witch crouched and set her briefcase and scepter on the ground. "We might as well do it right here and get this over with. I wouldn't want you to have a heart attack from tension in the meantime." Her words dripped with derisive venom.

Raven certainly has the best friends.

"You want to do some complicated ritual near a helipad at an airport?" Alison looked around, surprised. "Don't you think that will garner a little attention?"

"I have a certain understanding with certain local government officials if that's your concern. If we stay in this area, we'll be fine, and if there is an incident, I'll handle the aftermath with the authorities. They understand the importance of my work." A hint of pride filtered into her eyes. "I'm a...minor celebrity of sorts around here. Sometimes being able to clean up mistakes is as important as being able to destroy people."

Alison shook her head. "No way."

Cassandra frowned. "Excuse me?"

"There's no way we're doing this here." She gestured toward a plane parked in the distance. "This is an airport. I won't risk trouble at an airport. It's not a huge airport, but there's a risk of innocent people getting hurt. Do you want to know the difference between my company and some random mercenaries? We care if innocent people are hurt."

The witch sighed dramatically and shook her head, annoyance written all over her face. "Do you have reason to believe there will be trouble? Were you followed?"

"No." She lifted the box. "But given what this is, there's a strong possibility that we could have been, and we can't let our guard down until it's taken care of."

Cassandra picked up her briefcase and scepter. "Fine.

There's another location a few miles from here I use some-times—a field." Annoyance leaked from every word.

Alison nodded at the helicopter. "You should have simply had us meet you there, to begin with, rather than a damned airport."

"In my experience, large, public areas reduce the amount of trouble. Cockroaches like to avoid the light."

"In my experience, they only lead to more collateral damage. Sometimes, you deal with rabid bears and not cockroaches." She gestured toward the helicopter. "Let's go."

———

The empty field bordered by a crumbling fence satisfied Alison far more than the airport, even if Cassandra spent the brief flight looking like she had swallowed needles. It was as if flying a few miles away was the greatest inconvenience in the world.

I have the feeling she wouldn't even care if a fight started at the airport and someone was hurt. I don't care how many connections she has or how much of a local celebrity she is. I won't gamble with people's lives.

Alison shook her head at the thought. Her recent experiences with Andrei and Raven had made her think a little more deeply about what separated her from her enemies, and one big difference was her desire to protect people. It was why she had started a security company, and she never wanted to lose sight of that.

Everyone emptied out of the helicopter and followed Cassandra as she marched farther into the field, her briefcase and scepter in hand, and her irritated expression grew with each step. About twenty yards out, she halted abruptly and took a deep breath before she crouched and looked expectantly at them.

"Is this acceptable?" she asked. She nodded to a few trees that swayed in the wind in the distance. "There might be squirrels hibernating under a tree. I wouldn't want to risk their lives."

"This is fine," Alison muttered.

The witch snapped open the locks on the briefcase and raised the lid. Inside, various crystals of different sizes and colors lay embedded in soft gray foam inserts. She selected a few and set them in front of her. After a few more placements, it became clear that she formed the rough outline of a glyph with the different crystals.

I'm surprised she doesn't do this ritual at her place, but if she has everything she needs in that briefcase, it makes some sense. It certainly makes her more flexible.

"Once I begin the ritual, I'll have to continue to the end," the witch explained. "I can stop briefly to talk, but only briefly, and canceling it requires a number of measures that also take some time. So please, don't bother me until I'm finished unless you prefer me to die and a large explosion."

Alison stared at Cassandra, her mouth agape. That level of risk was even more of a reason to not have done it at the airport. Disgust washed through her.

Once she'd shaken her head and walked away, she gestured for her friends to come closer. "We're in a field, but we're not exactly in the middle of nowhere." She pointed in the distance toward a highway they'd flown over. "And there still is a chance someone might portal in, so stay alert. We obviously can't depend on Cassandra caring about anyone."

The others nodded and spread out around the witch.

A couple of minutes passed in silence as the woman arrayed sixty-four crystals in a precise pattern. Her hands moved quickly and precisely during the process, and she didn't bother to explain any of the steps. From what Alison could tell, she was setting up some sort of overly complicated portal spell. It wasn't like anything Alison had ever seen.

The witch raised the scepter and began to chant again in Enochian. Several of the crystals lit up, and their ethereal light bathed the area. A melodic hum filled the air. Soon, other crystals activated to add a ghostly harmony. Waves of magic pulsed from the wand and crystals. Alison's skin tingled.

I wonder where she got all those crystals. If each is an artifact, that represents a lot of effort or money.

"Alison, there might be an issue," Tahir reported over the link.

"I spotted it first," Sonya followed. "I want it noted for the record how cool I am. I beat Tahir."

"Duly noted," Alison responded. "But what is it exactly?"

"A large helicopter coming from the airport," he explained. "I checked on the drone's camera feed, and the chopper was parked but it took off a little after you did."

She frowned and searched the horizon. A dark dot grew in size in the direction of the airport, accompanied by a characteristic rhythmic thump in the distance but increasing in volume.

"Damn it," she muttered. "So much for this ending as an aerial tour of Washington." She headed to Cassandra. "We have trouble coming. We need to get you out of here."

The witch shook her head. She stopped her chant and wiped the sweat off her forehead. "I already told you this isn't something I can abandon. If there's trouble, deal with it. That's what you're paid for, isn't it?"

Alison sighed and nodded. She jogged in the direction of the approaching helicopter. "It might not be what we think. No one do anything stupid until we confirm there's trouble." She lowered her arms to her sides but didn't summon any shadow blades. There was no reason to look like a psycho if it turned out the new arrivals weren't enemies.

The rest of the team positioned themselves defensively. Drysi held her hand in her jacket while Hana gripped the *tachi*'s hilt. Mason was the only one who didn't reach for his weapon, but he'd already increased his strength.

A tense couple of minutes passed as the black dot grew into a blob and finally into a large cargo helicopter. It lowered itself to the ground, the wind from the blades swirling dust around it. The side door opened to reveal eight men in blue coveralls and blue hats with a corporate logo Alison recognized. The team hopped out of the helicopter and looked relaxed.

The vehicle rose once again and turned to depart.

Not exactly a high-tempo tactical insertion.

"Your ride's leaving," Alison commented. "Tahir, keep a drone on that thing," she whispered.

"On it," he responded through her receiver.

One of the men advanced, an easy smile under his dark

mustache. "Yeah. They have something else to take care of. But don't worry about them. Worry about yourself. Is your radio busted?"

Mason glanced at her and shook his head. She raised a hand to tell him to let her handle the situation.

"No," she replied. "Why do you ask?"

"We've tried to contact you since you took off. You've been leaking something. That's not a good thing." The man's gaze focused on Mason. "It surprised me that you didn't have a million alarms going off. Maybe your pilot didn't pay attention." He frowned as if in thought. "Oh, wait, is that why you're here? Lucky we decided to follow you."

Mason's expression darkened. "There's nothing wrong with our helicopter, and since when do we need eight mechanics to fix one random chopper?"

The man chuckled. "Don't get prickly, friend. We happened to be flying toward the airport and our guy noticed your leakage. We thought we'd help you out. You're the one in some random field."

Alison nodded, a forced smile on her face. Tahir's information indicated the man was lying. There was also the low-level magic she sensed around all of them. She might believe a magical mechanic, but not eight magical mechanics.

Their spokesperson cleared his throat. "So if you're not having trouble, what exactly are you doing here?"

"That's not your business," she interjected. "We're handling something—I suppose you could call it disposal—and she has all the appropriate...uh, burn permits." She pointed to dark clouds in the distance. "And it looks like it'll rain soon anyway."

Yeah, that's such a lame lie, Alison. It's December, not June.

The mustached man shook his head. "Maybe we should take a look at your helicopter to be sure. I would hate to see you lift off and crash." He frowned at Cassandra. "And you said you were burning something? It looks like she's doing some magic, and there are rules about doing many types of magic too close to the airport. You better stop, or there'll be trouble."

"Who will stop us?" Alison scrutinized them casually. "Aren't you supposed to be mechanics, not cops?"

His smile didn't reach his eyes. "Do we need to call the cops? I tried to cut you a break, but if you want to be a bitch about it, I don't mind seeing your ass in jail. I take airport safety very seriously."

She laughed. "You don't understand any of this, do you?"

Cassandra continued her chant and the haunting music grew even louder. Two bright points of light appeared in front of her.

The man sighed and glanced at his friends before he nodded. They all drew wands, and a scowl replaced his frown.

Alison extended a shadow blade. Hana foxed out and drew her sword at the same time. Drysi had a knife out so quickly, Alison was half-convinced she had used some kind of quick-summon spell.

The revealed wizards backed away and many of them stared at Hana and her glowing tails.

They must have no idea who I am if they're more worried

about Hana. Then again, a woman with nine glowing tails and a big-ass sword and whose skin is red from a magic ring is kind freakier-looking than the barely perceptible shield I have over me.

"This doesn't have to go badly," the lead wizard protested, the scowl now entrenched on his face. "If you turn the box over, you can walk. We're only here to pick something up, not hurt anyone."

She shook her head. "You can't believe I'd agree to that."

He laughed. "Look, chick. We have eight guys, and you have four and some old potions witch. If you try to fight, you'll die."

Another bright point of light appeared in front of Cassandra. She continued her ritual and ignored the men.

The wizard frowned at her. "You better stop, bitch, if you know what's good for you."

Alison glared at him. "Brownstone Security isn't in the habit of walking away from jobs."

"Brownstone Security?" His mouth twitched. "I don't believe it. Surrender now, and you don't have to die. We're not here to kill you. We're only here to pick up the box."

"She'll finish her work." She stepped to cover Cassandra. "I don't care how much Tatum is paying you. You won't be able to spend it if you're dead."

"Kill both of the white-haired bitches first!" the wizard screamed.

All eight men pointed their wands and shouted an incantation. They launched eight fireballs at point-blank range. The blasts pelted Alison, and she stumbled back and hissed in pain, but the bulk of the energy had been absorbed by her layered shields.

A quick flick of Drysi's wrist sent a dagger into the flank of the wizards. The explosion scattered two of their adversaries but didn't kill them. Alison wasn't the only one who had a shield.

Hana's movement became a near-blur as she charged into the enemy ranks, Mason close beside her. She slashed with the *tachi* to slice through both a wizard's shield and his neck. The bodyguard pounded into another man and his empowered punch catapulted his target into the wet, overgrown grass of the field.

Alison didn't attack and instead, extended her shield wider to protect the witch. She trusted in her team to eliminate the enemy. The important thing now was to allow Cassandra to finish the ritual.

The lead wizard fired another larger fireball, and it exploded against her to strain her shield and scorch the nearby grass.

Drysi hurled another dagger, this one glowing white, into one of the wounded men's chest. The blade cut cleanly to reach his heart. A second dagger followed, and she completed the kill.

Mason snapped a man's neck with a kick before Hana impaled another wizard.

The cockiness drained from the lead wizard's face, and he charged Alison as he chanted and raised his wand. A bright column of white shot from the tip.

Oh, a light sword. I don't see that much these days. Nice, but too bad for you, asshole. You should have run when you had the chance.

She channeled more magic into her shields. Cassandra's chanting grew louder and faster, as did the music of the crystals. It was now like being in the middle of some heavenly concert.

The attacking man made it only a few more feet before Hana impaled him from behind, grim determination in her vulpine eyes. The fox yanked the blade out and watched dispassionately as he fell, already dead.

Alison surveyed the area with a frown and half-expected a police dropship or sirens in the distance, but she didn't see or hear anything. She glanced at Cassandra. A lattice of dozens of points of light, energy flowing among them, now floated in front of the woman.

"Eight bodies." She released her own energy-intensive shield around the witch. "I hope those connections you talked about aren't total crap."

The woman ceased her chant and looked at Alison with a heavy-lidded gaze. "Don't worry about them. It's time to finish this." She stared at the lattice of light, her breathing ragged before she raised the scepter and shouted a final short incantation.

A bright flash blinded the group.

CHAPTER THIRTEEN

Alison squinted. The music had stopped, replaced by a harsh, dissonant crackle. Jagged lines of cerulean and violent light stretched in front of Cassandra and framed a juddering portal. A dense purple mist filled the other side.

The witch smiled and set the scepter down. She snatched the box and hurled it through the portal, where it immediately disappeared into the purple mist. While the team watched, she retrieved the scepter and flourished it while she murmured something under her breath.

The portal vanished.

No one said anything for several seconds as a cool wind cut through the field.

"I thought you were supposed to neutralize the magic," Alison observed.

Cassandra began placing her crystals back into her briefcase. "I removed the danger, didn't I? It's neutralized in that it'll never harm anyone on Earth or Oriceran." As she removed the crystals, she revealed deep scorch marks beneath them.

She gestured to where the portal had been. "And where did you send the box? Whatever you did, it seemed a lot more elaborate than merely opening a portal to Oriceran, and I assume you weren't dumb enough to dump something super-dangerous there."

The witch scoffed. "Of course I didn't send it to Oriceran. That would be idiotic and irresponsible."

"The World in Between?" she asked. It shouldn't have been possible for a single witch to open a portal there, but the artifact crystals might have provided the juice she needed.

Cassandra shook her head. "No. The last thing I would ever do is risk sending something powerful to a place filled with dangerous exiles and spirits. The box and potion are…somewhere else."

"Do you care to be a little more specific?" She frowned, not at all happy with the vague response.

"I can't," she replied. "The place I sent it to doesn't have a name. I only know that everything sent there decays rather quickly. I've done experiments to verify that. Think of it as an extra-dimensional landfill."

Alison pinched the bridge of her nose. "More damned experiments. How do you know you're not basically declaring war on some alien dimension? I'm also sure there are probably a half-dozen laws about what you've just done, but there's nothing I can do about that now."

"War?" Cassandra had made it about halfway through gathering the crystals, irritation in her eyes. "It's a dead world. Its only use is disposal. I would know. I've done this since before you were born. It's only recently that certain authorities have accepted the wisdom of my approach."

"Sure." She shrugged. "Just dump random dangerous things on someplace you don't know much about. Nothing could possibly ever go wrong in that scenario." She snorted.

"It hasn't yet." The witch's smile was condescending and scratched at Alison's patience. "And it never will."

Why I do have a feeling that two years from now, I'll have to clean up after her?

Drysi cleared her throat. "I don't understand something."

"What now?" Cassandra muttered.

The Welsh witch pointed at one of the dead wizards. "You had your portal open to some random place that destroys evidence. Why didn't we dump the bodies there?"

Alison winced. Some of her new team member's old instincts remained strong.

The older woman's gaze cut to Alison. "That would have caused complications. I trust you realize that."

She nodded and sighed. "She's right, Drysi. It'll be easy to explain this away as a self-defense claim to the local authorities, but if we start destroying evidence, it'll get messy quickly." She pulled her phone out. "It's probably best I call the cops right now."

Cassandra shook her head. "I'll contact them myself. I have a procedure to follow when this kind of thing happens. It'll be easier if you let me handle it."

"Eight dead guys in a field isn't unusual for you?"

Cassandra smirked at her. "It's hardly unusual for you either, Dark Princess." She finished packing away the crystals and closed the briefcase. "I need you to get me back to the airport. There are people there I need to make aware of what happened, and the rest of the authorities will be contacted via them. I won't need you to stay for the aftermath."

"Then let's get you back." Alison gestured toward the vehicle and her team walked toward it. "Tahir, what happened to the helicopter our friends flew in on?"

"It headed to the airport," he explained. "Several men emerged from a nearby building. They are standing near the helicopter, but they haven't loaded onto it."

"Reinforcements," she muttered and shook her head. "Mason, you load everybody on the helicopter and wait here. I'll go ahead to the airport and have a little chat with our new potential friends."

He frowned. "Without backup?"

Her chest ached from a few minor burns and she took a moment to place her hand on the wound and cast a minor healing spell. One of the big weaknesses she had compared to the other trained Drow was her inability to heal quickly. Myna had suggested it was partially related to her inability to shape change like them, but Alison had enough power otherwise to take care of her wounds in a different way, and she still had a healing potion if she needed it.

"I'm not worried that these guys will hurt me, but if things get too tough, I'll pull back." She grew a pair of shadow wings and elevated. "I simply want to make sure these assholes aren't dogging us the entire way back."

A few minutes later, a group of surprised men looked up as Alison descended at a leisurely pace and smiled the entire time. They hadn't bothered with fake uniforms this time. Most wore thick jackets to ward off December's chill but definitely didn't do a good job of concealing their wand and gun holsters.

She waved as she touched down and an array of wands and pistols pointed at her. "Good afternoon, gentlemen. Is one of you in charge, or was the asshole with the mustache the one calling all the shots?"

A man holding a gun stepped away from the group, his dark eyes narrowed on her. "I'm Easton. I'm in command here."

"In command?" She surveyed the team. "Mercs, then? That means you're not some kind of crazy true believers. That makes this easier."

Easton offered her a cold grin. "We believe in getting paid."

Alison stuck her hands in her pocket. She had a few shield layers up, but she wasn't that worried about them attacking. If they hadn't fired at her immediately, that left the chance for her to talk them down.

"The other guys are dead," she explained. "We gave them their chance, but they thought they could win. They were wrong." She sighed. "This will sound so conceited, but it'll help. Do you know who I am?"

"Alison Brownstone," he replied. "Yes, I know who you are."

She nodded toward his gun. "And you thought a few wands and anti-magic bullets might be enough? I want you to think about that. I want you to really consider if your small group of guys are the people who have the extraordinary luck, skill, and power to win against me when so many other people and creatures have failed?"

Damn, this is embarrassing, even to me, but if it gets these idiots to back off, it's worth it.

The man snorted. "You had friends with you before. Now, you're alone. That's damned cocky, Brownstone. It'll probably get you killed. I admit my forward team underestimated yours, but now, we have the numbers and odds we need to win."

"Unless I slip and stab myself, that won't happen." She pulled her hands out of her pocket and he flinched. "During the last fight, I didn't do much because I had to protect someone and something from getting damaged, and my friends finished off all the other mercs, but here? Now? There's nothing I have to protect. That means I can go full out on you."

There's no reason to confirm to these guys that I don't want to fight at an airport.

"You're full of shit," Easton snarked.

Alison shrugged. "Most of my fights are a matter of public record." She sighed. "But let's talk about this from another angle. You were paid to get the box, right? If not the box, then the vial inside? Too late. We've already disposed of it."

"That's what you're going with?" He snorted.

"It's true. The only reason I flew back here and didn't immediately attack you is that I have no reason to unless you're an idiot." She gestured to the helicopter. "So you can leave. But if you're really aching to die, that's fine by me. I simply want to get it over with if that's how this will end."

No sirens, and no police. I wonder if that means they had something set up, or if it's something Cassandra already had set up.

A dull roar sounded in the distance over her shoulder. Alison glanced that way. A small jet approached the airport for a landing. She returned her attention to the merc.

"What'll it be?" Alison asked.

Easton grunted and holstered his gun. "Screw it. There's no money in it without the box." He stomped toward the helicopter.

The other men holstered their wands or guns and followed their leader, although a few glared at her.

She watched them for a moment before she jogged toward an open but empty hangar in the distance. While she wanted to rejoin her team, she also didn't want to distract the plane coming in for landing by flying away with her shadow wings.

Okay. We'll definitely get some victory sushi tonight.

CHAPTER FOURTEEN

O'Neil's phone rang again as the mercenary leaned up against a brick wall of the bar. A cigarette dangled from his lips. He'd received a text a few minutes prior informing him that he should be ready to take the call. Although he didn't like being told what to do, this particular caller usually made it worth his while.

The mercenary retrieved the device and brought to his ear. "Yeah? What did you need? I was having a good time tonight."

"Good times often require a fair amount of money, and I have a client who has need of your services," a familiar voice said through the phone, a corporate fixer he'd worked for in the past.

"What kind of service are we talking?" He took a long drag of his cigarette. "That last job you sent me in October went okay, but it wasn't the kind of thing I like to do. I'm not a fucking detective."

"One moment. Let me further secure the call."

A faint click sounded over the line.

"Are we good?" O'Neil asked.

"Yes," his contact replied. "This job is more suited to your natural talents. It's a search and destroy job in a rural area. There's a single target, a...magical with stealth and energy generation abilities. If he were a bounty, the target would easily be a class-five. He has heavy regeneration potential, so you'll need to eliminate him with excessive force."

"That sounds dangerous." He chuckled. "Why not simply bomb his ass?"

"The parties ultimately responsible would like this quieter than that. We need a tactical team who can be effective without drawing too much attention to the situation. And that's where you come in."

O'Neil took another drag of his cigarette. "Search and destroy, but you want this shit quiet. How quiet?"

"Quiet enough. There are some questions that don't need to be asked by certain people. These would be disruptive to certain established relationships that are profitable for everyone involved." The corporate fixer took a deep breath. "Including you, so we'd like you to put together an appropriate team that can eliminate the target without attracting too much notice. We'll have limited ability through certain contacts to keep certain interests away from your area of operation."

The merc grunted. "It sounds fun. Find some guy, kill him, and collect a paycheck. I like it when jobs are easy."

"Good. My representative will provide a full briefing in person in Portland. The target is currently in rural south-west Washington. This is a time-sensitive matter as his continued travel risks drawing too much of the aforementioned attention and questions."

He tossed his cigarette on the floor and stubbed it out with his boot tip. "You said quiet enough. What about witnesses or others in the area?"

Sometimes, his clients wanted him to avoid unnecessary collateral damage, whereas others didn't care or even actively encouraged it. A few years back, he'd even been paid to purposefully destroy a village while on another job so the local government could use the massacre for PR value.

O'Neil didn't care. He only cared about receiving compensation commensurate with the personal risks.

"I'll trust in your discretion," the other man explained. "There's a major bonus on this one. Someone really screwed up this time."

He snickered. "Good, I love cleaning up rich people's mistakes and having them pay me for it."

Alison's head swam from the sake, and she had trouble focusing. She knelt beside Mason in front of a low table in a private room in Maneki while Hana and Drysi sat on the other side. Tahir and Sonya had turned down the offer to join the event. Trays of every type of sushi and sashimi on the menu lay in front of them, along with several bowls of rice and two bottles of sake. It included every ingredient they needed for a victory sushi party.

Okay, maybe that's enough booze for tonight, she thought and blinked a few times in an effort to clear her vision.

She set her cup down and leaned against Mason, her cheeks warm. "I think we're cursed this month. Super-cursed."

He glanced at her and his lips curled into an amused smile. He was the designated driver for the night so experienced only the glories of a cold Coke rather than sake.

Hana finished swallowing some uni nigiri and frowned. "Cursed? We've kicked ass lately. What are you talking about? Since Vancouver, I think everything's gone great—maybe even the best it's gone in a while. We don't have to worry about dark wizards messing with us anymore, and they messed with everything we did."

Drysi's smile faltered. She had played some role in some of those dark wizard plots.

She does get that we trust her, right? I hope so.

The fox nodded toward the other woman. "And we have a new team member who says things like 'bloody' and 'tidy' in that cool accent."

The witch laughed and took a sip of her sake. "Bloody right."

"Now we only need a cool French chick," Hana suggested with a giggle. "We can call ourselves Mason's Babes."

He grimaced. "Wait? What? I think I'm happy with only the one babe."

Drysi snickered and gulped more alcohol.

Alison sighed. "A lot of good things have happened, but this month, we worked for a mobster and Mason's crazy and evil ex-girlfriend."

The two other women exchanged wicked grins and the bodyguard groaned again.

Hana nodded solemnly. "There's nothing worse than a Mason Babe who turns to the dark side. She makes a mockery of the entire Mason Babe Alliance."

"There is no Mason Babe Alliance," the man all but shouted.

Drysi threw her head back and cackled. "And there never will be with an attitude like that."

"Besides, it's not like we took the job to help Raven," Mason pointed out. "And now, she's left Seattle, hopefully for good. She might have had us help take care of that thing, but she's still the person responsible for creating the problem, to begin with."

"See, working for an evil Mason Babe," Alison muttered.

He sighed.

Drysi's face was now so flushed she might have been mistaken for using the defensive ring. "It doesn't matter. We stopped something nasty, and it was a right tidy job. All those bastards who came after us are dead, and we're all still alive." She slapped the table to rattle the trays and cups. "I wouldn't let it bother you so much, Alison. I don't think you could do the wrong thing even if you tried. You're too much of a bloody goody-two-shoes. All that power and you're always worried about saving everything else, including people who don't deserve it."

"I'm not a goody...shoe," Alison muttered, her head still on Mason's shoulder. "I simply want to...help people. Is that so wrong?" She sat up and blinked in irritation. "I can't be any other way. I don't want to be Queen of the Under-world, and I don't want to be Queen of the Drow. It sounds annoying. Power is annoying except when you're helping people."

"I'm not complaining." Drysi shrugged. She filled her cup with more sake. "Most people would have killed me a long time ago, but you gave me a job and are helping me do something decent with my life."

Hana nodded quickly but said nothing as her mouth was full of tuna sashimi. She managed to smile around her food.

"I, for one, like that you care so much, A," Mason interjected. "It's one of the things that attracted me to you, the true Mason Babe."

The witch snorted. "Bloody men. Even when you're nice you can't help but lie."

He frowned. "What am I lying about?"

Drysi pointed at Alison. "She's not exactly ugly now, is she? A beautiful young woman who is rich and a powerful magical." She leaned forward, her eyes unfocused as she looked at Alison. "It's not like it's some hardship to snog someone like that, now is it?"

Something approaching panic appeared on Mason's face. Alison tried not to laugh, but it slipped out.

"They initially saw each other in the gym," Hana mock-whispered. "So that means when he first saw her, she was always in tight clothes."

Some distant part of Alison's mind suggested she should be embarrassed, but the alcohol haze kept it contained. She laughed again, but she wanted to poke her friend a little.

"You're the one who was always obsessed with sexy gym outfits," she slurred. "My selections are based on functional. I wasn't trying to get a man."

Wow. I'm drunk. It's been a while since I've let myself relax enough to get drunk, but it's not so bad. Mason's sober, and I know he'll always protect me.

Mason watched the women, his face tight and his arm around his girlfriend's waist.

The fox snickered as she filled a bowl with rice with her chopsticks and lifted it toward her mouth. "If you'd had your Brownstone Security gym ready from the beginning, you might not have ever met your man."

Alison managed a chuckle. "That's a good point, but I did get him, and I love him."

"I love you too, A," he replied.

Drysi shook her head. "Bloody love birds." She took another sip of her drink.

No one spoke for the next minute or so as they downed more sushi, rice, and drinks.

Hana eyed Alison after she'd swallowed a bite of rice and set down her bowl and chopsticks. "Since we're in a good mood here, I wanted to double-check if it's okay to bring Omni to work. I think he would be good for team morale. The fish aren't impressive enough. Even the glowing ones." She nodded knowingly.

Alison sat up and frowned. She rubbed her temples and tried to focus on her memories. Something didn't sit right with Hana's statement. "Wait, I thought I said I didn't want Omni brought to work. I didn't want pets becoming a thing there. I said that, didn't I?"

Mason and Drysi nodded their confirmation.

The fox snapped their fingers. "It was worth a try but think about it. He might become really helpful. He changes shape. We could put bugs on him or something and have him deliver them in rat or ferret mode, or he can turn into a bird and become a living drone."

"You can't make him change on command," Alison replied. "And trust me, it's too dangerous. The last thing anyone with the last name Brownstone would ever do is place someone's pet in danger unless we're looking to destroy an entire organization."

Mason chuckled. "She's only trying to think of excuses to bring Omni to work, A. I don't think she's serious." His smile faltered. "You aren't, right?"

The woman shook a finger at them. "You don't know what I'm serious about. Fine. No Omni at Brownstone Security." She scoffed. "You're probably part of King Oriceran's conspiracy. You can tell His Royal Highness that he will never have Omni."

She laughed. "I'm part of the conspiracy?"

"Maybe?" Hana swayed slightly, her cheeks rosy.

"That would be impressive since I don't even know about it."

The fox leaned back, her eyes narrowed. "Okay, maybe you aren't part of the conspiracy."

Drysi picked up her sake cup. "We should toast."

"I'm not toasting to the conspiracy," Hana complained.

The witch laughed. "Not to the conspiracy."

"To what?" Alison asked and raised her head from Mason's shoulder.

"To Omni!" Drysi shouted. "May he forever change shape and make Hana happy."

The nine-tailed fox's eyes widened in delight, and she

whipped up her cup but spilled some the contents in her enthusiasm. "To the best damned pet ever, Omni!"

Mason chuckled and raised his cup. "To Omni."

Alison smiled warmly. Her earlier concerns slid into the abyss of disregard. She reminded herself of the good things. Her company was growing. In a sense, her family was growing. She was making a difference in the world, and she'd helped stop a dangerous potion from hurting people and turned a man away from crime. That wasn't a cursed December. It was a good December.

It's almost Christmas. We'll have a great time visiting my family, and I doubt anything as obnoxious as working for Raven will come up. What are the chances of me having to clean up someone else's big mistake again that quickly?

CHAPTER FIFTEEN

Chilly rain poured from the dark clouds in a relaxing rhythm against the pavement. The droplets bounced off the small shield Alison had conjured above her head. She stepped into the lobby of the Brownstone Security building and her gaze cut to the massive fish tank.

Hana wanted the thing so badly, but now she has Omni, she doesn't care. Oh, well. It's not like I'm the one who has to clean it.

Sienna sat at the front desk and typed at her computer. She looked up with a bright smile. "Welcome back. Was your coffee okay?"

"It was good. Sometimes, it's good to have a cup away from the office." She shrugged.

"Sure. I totally understand." The woman smiled and returned to her work.

Alison waved and continued past the massive front desk to the hallway leading to her office. Her phone rang after she entered, almost as if the caller could sense her location, but that wasn't a concern in the heavily warded building.

Curiosity rather than concern filled Alison as she grabbed the phone from the pocket of her red denim jacket. Her original she'd brought with her to Seattle had long since met its end, but she liked the style and had purchased a new one. It was functional and fun. She would never have the obsession with flirty and sexy clothes like Hana, but that didn't bother her, nor did it seem to bother Mason.

It's nice to be loved for who I am. Exactly like Mom loves Dad for who he is.

Alison's smile vanished when she saw the caller ID. She'd forgotten the number was even in her phone.

INCOMING CALL: RUBY SUMNER.

Ruby Sumner, the human disguise of Rasila, the Drow Princess of the Endless Shadow.

She groaned and closed her office door behind her before she answered the call. Avoiding an annoyance would only make it return at an even more vexing time.

"Hello, Ruby," Alison answered.

"Hello, Alison," Rasila answered cheerfully. "It's been far too long since we last chatted. We should get together for lunch. How about today? There's a new cherry pie I wanted to try at this bakery downtown. Everyone says it's as delicious as you'll achieve without magic."

Alison frowned and didn't answer immediately. Was lunch some sort of code for a duel? If it was the duel, what did cherry pie mean? A duel to the death? Before, Rasila had insisted that such a duel would be inappropriate between Drow princesses, but she didn't trust the woman given the complicated scheme she had concocted a couple of months prior.

"Alison, are you still there?" the Drow pressed.

"Yes, Ruby. I was merely confused by lunch. I wondered if that meant anything else."

"No. Lunch. Not brunch." She laughed softly. "You know, lunch. The meal you generally eat in the middle of the day, but obviously, schedules do vary. If you want to call it something else, I don't care."

"And cherry pie?" Alison snorted. "Do you expect me to think you, of all people, want to try a new cherry pie?"

"You sound tense. It's probably because you don't eat enough pie." A faint hint of mockery crept into Rasila's voice. "Somehow, public and popular limits certain negative possibilities, especially given our mutual situations. I would have thought you would approve of my choice."

"Fine," she muttered. "I'll meet you. Text me the time and address."

She's right. If she wanted to set a trap up, attacking me in the middle of the city when AET would show up doesn't make much sense. But there's something going on here, and I'd better find out what.

Rasila sat across from Alison, her hands folded neatly over the glass table in the center of the tightly packed room. She wore her human shape today, an attractive dark-haired woman in her twenties with a mole on her cheek. Her short, tight blue dress was an odd choice given the weather, but Alison was hardly one to criticize fashion choices, especially given her best friend.

Tahir observed the whole thing via cameras inside the

bakery dining room. Hana, Drysi, and Mason sat parked one block down in a company SUV. If it were a trap, Rasila would be caught in it.

Silence hovered over the table. Alison had summoned a bubble to protect their conversation shortly after they settled. Rasila followed up with a spell that randomized their mouth movements from the outside perspective after mentioning that "humans have so many spying toys, even without magic."

Alison's annoyance built as she brought another piece of the cherry pie to her mouth and bit it off the fork. It was a perfect balance of tanginess and sweetness with good texture on the crust and a hint of almond.

Damn it. She did pick a good place. That really pisses me off. She's not Myna. She understands Earth and Earth culture, and that makes her dangerous.

"You're so quiet, Alison," Rasila commented after she swallowed a mouthful of her pie. "What do you think of it?"

"It's...good," she muttered. "Very good. Probably some of the best cherry pie I've had in a while."

Her companion offered her a lop-sided smile. "You have no reason to hate me."

"You hired me so you could purposefully ambush me. That's not the kind of thing to build a friendship on. It's a straight-up bitch move."

"I did it to test you, and why are you complaining? You defeated both me and my underlings." The Drow snorted. "I should be the one who is upset, but I'm not because there's no dishonor in being defeated by a superior foe. I look past that and into the future."

Alison set her fork down. "What's this about? Do you want another duel?"

Rasila shook her head. She stared at Alison for a moment, her lips slightly parted. "I have no reason to believe it would end any differently."

"You could cheat. You could set up another ambush." She shrugged.

"Weak trickery. I'm not a coward like Widow Maker." Rasila snorted. "You should know that it was very satisfying to me to find out that not only was she slain, but she was slain by humans and not even magicals." She laughed. "I can't think of a more fitting end for that creature. She was always driven by such base passions, yet her loyalty to Laena was unrelenting, and so she was accorded more status than she should have been." Bitterness crept into her voice near the end. She waved off the approaching waitress.

Alison frowned at the mention of the Drow assassin. The Widow Maker had been Laena's first major attempt to recover Alison, and neither the assassin nor the former Drow Queen cared if the plan involved the potential deaths of her adopted mother and father.

Rasila dug her fork into her pie. "Humans are so fascinating. I don't think Drow could ever make a fruit pie with so many fascinating layers of flavor. There are downsides to being overly fond of meat." She lifted the fork. "There's no secret plot here, Alison, not in the sense that you think. I want to get to know you better. As I hope you now appreciate, I've spent enough time on Earth that human culture and activities aren't confusing to me, but you are, and you're half-human. Your Drow half isn't responsible for your behavior, and your human side isn't either, from what I've seen. The more I think about what happened between us, the more puzzled I am."

"I don't get it. Because I didn't kill you?" Alison shrugged. "Plenty of humans are merciful. It's the cornerstone of a lot of human religions."

The other woman finished another bite. "Humans are not so different than Drow. Power is something they seek and is at the center of their countless petty little wars."

"Not everyone is obsessed with power," she replied. "Most people aren't."

"Because most people are weak, especially humans." Rasila sighed and shook her head. "What value is there in worrying about power when you're weak? It's nothing but a dream of self-destruction or servitude."

Alison sighed. "If that's how you think, you might never understand me, then. I simply don't think like you. I feel that I've been blessed with power, and I want to use it to protect other people. I don't really worry about gaining more power, either personal or political."

"That's a conceit of someone already powerful." Rasila scoffed. "It's arrogant in a way, but I haven't come to insult you, Princess of the Shadow Forged."

"Then what have you come to do, other than share admittedly delicious pie with me?"

"I came to warn you." She sighed as her fork met her plate and glanced down. She'd finished her slice.

"Warn me about what?" Alison asked. "I know you have underworld connections, but I also know they are shallower than they could be. Being able to interact with the underworld isn't the same thing as controlling it."

"Oh, is that what Vincent tells you? Or Raven?" Rasila raised a dark eyebrow.

She snorted. "Am I supposed to be impressed? And whatever happened to calling Widow Maker a coward for sneaking around?"

The Drow frowned for the first time in the conversation. "She's a coward because she didn't face her true foes as herself. It's not the same thing. I would never take the shape of one of your loved ones to try to trap you. That's beneath me." Her nostrils flared, and she narrowed her eyes. "But no matter. I'm not here to warn you about the Seattle underworld or whatever sad wizards you're destroying this month. The threat is something very Oriceran. The other three princesses are beginning to stir, and my spies have heard talk that you are their current main concern." She snickered before she reached over to grab Alison's plate and her half-eaten slice of pie. "Everyone has learned that you defeated me. Word of your involvement with the exile Myna has also spread." She took a bite of her stolen dessert.

Alison tossed her fork on the table and folded her arms. "They are concerned about me?"

Rasila nodded.

"The one person who has loudly and repeatedly said she doesn't want to be queen?" she asked.

"Of course. You're an unknown factor. When Laena consolidated power, she pushed most of the princesses away and made sure they could never truly unseat her. None of us dared challenge her, so there was little reason to undermine each other during that time. But none of us anticipated her reign would collapse so quickly because of outside influence, and even though we didn't attack each other throughout the reign of the former queen, that doesn't mean we didn't study each other to learn weaknesses. All the princesses know how to counter each other, but you..." She offered a lop-sided smile. "Some think you'll repeat your adopted father's path and come to wreak a terrible vengeance upon us when we least expect it. Others think you will seize control after we've destroyed each other. Novati believes that your company is an attempt to build an army or at least a personal guard to use when you decide to take power."

"Novati," Alison echoed. "The Princess of the Dark Sun. When I was on Oriceran, everyone said she was almost as ruthless as Laena."

"That's accurate. She didn't let herself fall into the petty and venal corruption of our former queen, but you'll find she is much harder to reason with than me. If anyone would simply attempt to kill you, it would be her. She still honors some of the ways, however, and that should keep her from murdering you anytime soon unless she has much greater reason to believe you're about to make a strong move toward becoming the queen. Drae, the Princess of the Deepest Night, is the one who might most likely undermine you with games."

"Games?"

Rasila sighed as she finished the last bite of her stolen pie. "She lacks the sheer direct strength of Novati or me, but she's a clever one, and she's also not above using outsiders to help her."

She nodded. "I heard the same thing when I was on Oriceran. A lot of Drow seemed to dislike her for that."

"They do, but they also admire power." She pushed the empty plate back toward her. "And they will follow her if they believe she can win."

"But what about the Guardians?"

"They are fragmented and weak." Rasila snorted blatant disdain. "They have no ability to eliminate the princesses without seeming like tyrants and sparking a war, and they must spend their resources and time monitoring all of us. The only one they don't care about is you."

"Good. At least someone understands I'm not involved in this."

"It marks them as short-sighted fools. They should at least attempt to curry your favor as a shield against the other princesses. The fact that they don't proves they are too foolish to rule the Drow."

She shook her head. "I'm happy someone is leaving me out of this. What about Miar? When I was there, I heard a lot of interesting things about her—such as she was somewhat in support of the Guardians."

Rasila's face scrunched in disgust. "The Princess of the Soul Shadow's people are very loyal to her out of love, not fear, but she's a lot like you. She lacks ambition. I often wonder if it's because she's the oldest and so believed for a longer time she had no chance to be queen. Supporting the pathetic Guardians is only proof of her weakness."

Alison shrugged. "It sounds like she won't mess with me."

"That's not true at all."

"Why wouldn't it be?" Alison blinked.

"Because I've spent time spreading tales of your power and the confidence and the skill of your underlings." Rasila's triumphant smile made her want to stab the woman with a shadow blade. "She worries about you as much as the others because you could disrupt everything, and you're too strong to easily ignore. She cares as much about the future of the Drow as I do, whereas the other two care more about themselves."

"I only have your word about that."

"I don't deny I would personally benefit from being queen, but that doesn't make anything else I've said any less true."

"Maybe." She narrowed her eyes and her face heated. "And if anyone attacks my people because you've riled them up, I'll hold you personally responsible."

The Drow's dismissive snort only made Alison's face heat more. "No one will attack your people. Miar would find that beneath her, and the other two are overly concerned about your reaction. I've also made it very clear that you are willing to accept personal duels, but should they attempt anything that involves killing your under-lings, they'll earn the wrath of not only you but potentially your father as well. After all, he's famous for annihilating hundreds for the murder of his pet."

"They're worried about Dad?" She grinned. "I like that. I can use that."

"Did they ever tell you what some call your father in our language? I imagine some would be too afraid to do that."

"Destroyer of Queens."

Rasila uttered a throaty laugh. "I've also done my best to spread the word of what happened in Vancouver, and I've made it clear that your army goes far beyond only the employees of Brownstone Security. A princess who makes you a true enemy is liable to be destroyed, or so they believe."

Alison let the revelations sink in for a few moments. "If I understand this right, you've riled them up enough that they might come after me personally, at least for a duel, but you've gone out of your way to make sure they don't hurt my people."

"A mostly accurate summary."

"Why? Wouldn't it be to your advantage for them to eliminate my people? It would weaken my position."

The Drow snorted. "You might think I care only about myself, but I do care about the future of our people, and that future will need to involve both Earth and Oriceran. Even if you aren't queen, you have a unique insight into that relationship. I won't toss aside or alienate a useful resource so easily, nor will I allow the others to do so. We will not repeat the short-sighted mistakes of Laena."

She nodded slowly. "And do you think any of them will actually challenge me?"

"I can't know for certain, but I believe you're safe for at least a month. Perhaps a few, but not much longer than that. They will make a move of some sort, whether a direct challenge or something more underhanded."

"And it won't help if I swear that I don't want to be queen?" She allowed some desperation to show in her face and her voice.

Rasila shook her head. "Events are moving past our mere desires. But know this, Alison. We might never be friends, but I'll do my best to ensure we're not enemies."

She released a long sigh. The princess promised a

month or two of peace, but soon, Alison wouldn't be able to escape Drow politics. If she traveled to Oriceran and challenged them directly, that might only result in more destabilization or harm the efforts of the Guardians to smooth the transition of power, which would only mean more trouble for her.

I'll have a good time at Christmas. Next year sounds like it'll be busy.

CHAPTER SIXTEEN

Alison crept up her stairs and the wood creaked under her feet. The soft patter of rain on the roof sounded from above. She'd helped herself to a little snack before heading to bed. Mason already snored peacefully on his side of the bed, although he'd deny in the morning, as he always did. He unhesitatingly stated every time that he never snored. It was too much fun to tease a life wizard about something so small.

The earlier conversation with Rasila haunted her, if only because it brought back thoughts of Myna's sacrifice. The ancient Drow seemed convinced Alison should be queen, and it was hard to ignore the possibility that on a certain level, she'd sacrificed her life for that reason—something Alison insisted would never happen.

I don't want to be queen, but do I owe it to Myna to at least help make sure the Drow situation is stable? If there's civil war and people die, it's hard for me to simply sit back and say it's not my problem when it was my dad who took Laena down because he was mad about her attempts to kidnap me.

The more I think about it, the less strange it is that the Drow are all obsessed with me.

She stopped at the top of the stairs, her hand resting on the wooden railing, and sighed. It was something she would worry about after Christmas. There was no use in obsessing over a problem she couldn't resolve in the next couple of weeks.

The door to Sonya's room inched open, and the blonde teen poked her head out, a curious look on her face.

Alison smiled at her and liked how her current hairstyle framed her face. The teenager had grown her hair over the last few months. She thought it looked good, but she also wanted to support any non-damaging choice Sonya made. If she'd said she wanted to shave it, she would have supported that, too. The girl had years of confidence she needed to recover, and one place to start was with little things like autonomy over her appearance.

"Hey, Alison," she began, her voice quiet. "Can we talk for a minute?"

She nodded. "Sure." Without hesitation, she headed toward the girl's room.

A comfortable-looking black rolling chair sat in front of a large glass desk in one corner of the room. Three screens rested on the surface, with the main computer underneath. A number of peripheral interface devices for Sonya's wand lay to the side of her keyboard.

The only other pieces of furniture were the queen-sized bed in the corner and a plain brown nightstand. No matter how much Alison prodded, her ward still seemed averse to decorating her room beyond the bare minimum. She wanted her to feel like it was home, but she didn't want to stress her out over it either.

Sonya sat in the chair, her hands folded in her lap. She was still in her hoodie and jeans from earlier in the day.

Alison moved to the bed and sat on the edge. "What did you want to talk about?"

The girl took a deep breath and looked at Alison, although she struggled visibly to maintain eye contact. "It's only…with Christmas coming up and everything, I thought I should thank you."

She frowned a little. "For what exactly?"

"I don't know. Like everything?" Sonya shrugged. "I already thanked Tahir and Hana the other day, but I live in your house. Before, I lived in your condo. You didn't have to do that. You could have put me into the system. And you've given me a job, so I'm saving up a lot of money while I learn from Tahir."

"It's not a big deal." Alison smiled. "And I know a little something about what it means to lose your parents and have someone step up to help you."

"Losing your parents, huh?" The teenager lowered her head. "Sometimes, I think about tracking my dad down. Tahir's taught me a lot of crap, and my hacking and magic skills are a lot stronger than they used to be, maybe better than my dad's. I'm starting to think he wasn't that good, to begin with, especially compared to Tahir. I bet I could find him."

She nodded. "You could. Do you want to live with him again?"

That was one plan she couldn't support after what the

man had done, but she wanted to talk it through with Sonya.

The girl's lips curled in a sneer. "No way. I hate that bastard. I want to mess with him, not kill him, but at least make him feel some pain. Maybe get him arrested wherever he is."

"I can relate to that." She didn't elaborate. Sonya already knew the truth about what happened to Alison's biological father, but there was no reason to linger on his death. "But I can also tell you that the best way to deal with those kinds of negative emotions is to move on from them."

Sonya sighed. "But how? I try not to think about him, but when I do, I get so pissed off. It's not like he was a great dad, but he could at least have not left me to get smacked around."

Alison took a deep breath. "The best way to handle it is to focus on the people you have around you now who do care about you." She smiled. "That's what I did—my new dad and mom and my friends and professors at the School of Necessary Magic. When you do that, the negative feelings you have begin to fade, and you don't let the people who hurt you live in your head forever. The past is what it is, and in my life and professional experience, pieces of garbage end up with the rest of the trash. The kind of man who would abandon his daughter is definitely a piece of garbage."

Her companion rubbed her wrist. "I understand that I have good people helping me. I'll try to think about you all more and less about how that bastard left or my mom."

She stood and walked over to pull Sonya into a hug. "We'll keep helping you, Sonya. You don't ever have to worry about any of those people ever again. You do understand that, right?"

"Yeah." She hugged her in return. "Thanks again, Alison."

Fifteen minutes later, Alison was back downstairs on her couch, her phone in hand. The discussion of the past had brought up different memories. For all her talk of moving on from the past, she'd lived there far longer than Sonya.

It's late, but she might still be awake.

Alison dialed and held her breath, her heart pounding. There was no reason to be nervous about a simple phone call.

"Hey, Alison," Izzie answered with a yawn. "Is everything okay? We talked only a few days ago."

"Everything's fine." She sighed. "Sorry. I don't even know where you are and how late it is there. Did I wake you?"

"Don't worry. I was asleep, but I'm spending some time with my parents right now. It's not like they'll complain if I sleep in a little." Her friend laughed. "And It feels good, actually."

"Sleeping in?"

"No, you calling. I like the idea that my friends can call me whenever they want to and chat about whatever they feel like. It definitely beats me having to set up some bullshit meeting via magic self-destructing letters and worry about dark wizards hurting them." Izzie blew out a breath. "I feel so free. It's hard to explain how it feels after years of having those bastards looming over me and always worried about them getting me. I even joked about going on a vacation with my parents now that all their latest crap is taken care of. Something silly, like an amusement park." She laughed. "My dad seemed really enthusiastic about the idea. He always does like the oddest things about Earth."

"I was thinking about the past and definitely not amusement parks." Alison laughed. "And after I just got done telling Sonya to focus on the present and the future. I'm such a hypocrite."

"The past helps determine the present, and the present helps determine the future." Izzie chuckled ruefully. "My past screwed me for a long time, but I'm interested in the future and what I can get out of it. There are so many opportunities. Almost too many. It's hard to know which way to go."

"My offer still stands," she mentioned.

"You tell me that every time, but I can't bring myself to do it. I would love to spend more time with you, but I also need a break for a while, from…all of it." Her friend sighed. "From the very beginning at school, there was no true innocence, not with what they did to my memories. I understand why they did it, but still." She fell silent for a few seconds. "Sometimes, I think about doing what your dad did—leaving the bounty hunting and violence mostly behind to take up something else. I simply don't know what it would be. I did nothing but focus on hunting dark wizards and bounties to support myself. I don't know how to live a normal life."

"But you can learn. You have the opportunity now." Alison chuckled when a brutal truth confronted her. "But you're right. I'm many things, but not a woman living a normal life. I never have been and whatever chance I had for that ended with what happened with my birth mom."

"You're not angry with me about not wanting to join your company, are you?" Izzie asked.

"No, I want you to be happy, and if you're happier finding yourself away from the kind of lifestyle I lead, then good." She took a deep breath and exhaled slowly. "But there's another person you used to know who doesn't have a violent lifestyle anymore. At least most of the time."

Her friend grew quiet again, her breathing shallow but audible. "I have called Luke if that's what you're getting at."

"He still loves you," Alison insisted. "I know he does."

"And I've told you before I don't think I can return any of that," Izzie replied. "We've talked and even had dinner a few times. It was…awkward but relaxing in a weird way. It was like watching an old movie you used to love but can't quite capture that same enjoyment. I haven't ruled anything out but I think, like you and Tanner, I can't go back to what I had, no matter how much I want to. I'm still adjusting to life and maybe I should settle down with some nice, non-magical accountant and get a job in a tree nursery or something. I would never have thought of anything like that before."

"You have time. You should try whatever you want or travel the world without the pressure of the dark wizards."

"I might actually do that." She yawned again.

"You should go to sleep. It was rude of me to call you at night."

"I'm okay."

Alison smiled at her phone. "And I am too now. I think I

wanted to hear a voice that reminded me things can get better."

"Anytime you need to call me, Alison, you can. We have years to make up for having to go months without talking."

She could almost hear the grin through the phone.

"Same for me, whether you want to hang out or you need help with trouble," she replied.

"I hope I never again need the amount of help I had in Vancouver," her friend added, a hint of amazement in her voice. "If I do, I've done something very wrong. I'll talk to you again soon, Alison. Take care of yourself. I hope you have a good Christmas."

"Same to you, Izzie."

The call ended, and she lowered the phone slowly.

We can't change the past, but we can make the future better. What's the end for me? Dad was closing in on twenty years as a bounty hunter when he decided to open the restaurant. Will I do this kind of thing for twenty years?

Sometimes, I wonder. Finishing off the Seventh Order and scaring the dark wizards into behaving means I had my revenge, too.

She looked over her shoulder at the stairs. The future slept upstairs in both Sonya and Mason.

It's tiring, but I do like my life, although I could use a few less Drow princesses and crazy, evil exes of my boyfriend showing up.

CHAPTER SEVENTEEN

O'Neill's boots sank into the muddy forest floor and pulled out with a soft sucking sound. Despite it being early in the morning, the cloudy sky and dense towering firs and pines combined to force a near twilight atmosphere as the mercenary and his three associates traveled through the trees. The gloom was oppressive but appropriate for hunting a monster. His anti-magic deflector bounced lightly against his chest.

The recent rain had made it harder to track the test subject, but they knew he was in the area. His tracking beacon had pinged several times, which was surprising because according to his team's briefing, beacon activity had been sporadic to almost non-existent since the man had made his escape from the lab.

The hungry mud also denied the merc the use of an exoskeleton. He couldn't risk being stuck in the unstable terrain, but it didn't matter. Between the anti-magic bullets and grenades available, it would be more than enough to defeat the target. Blow anyone into enough pieces, and it didn't matter if they could regenerate. They merely needed to find the target first.

O'Neill swept his gun in a wide arc as he peered into the dense undergrowth, eager to find and kill their quarry. His client had even gone to the trouble of supplying his team with several anti-magic magazines. Not having to use his own meant it would be a very profitable day, especially since he hadn't had to recharge his anti-magic deflector on his last job.

"What you got, Jones?" he asked the large man wearing AR goggles on his right. The other man also carried a rifle and a backpack, but the two on either side held wands. The mercenary had learned that when fighting magicals, you should always bring a magical. Although, in this case, the target wasn't technically a full magical. His client had been a little less forthcoming on the exact identity of the target, but he had at least related his capabilities.

Not knowing didn't bother him. Fairly soon, the target would be dead, so his true identity would become irrelevant. After all, that was why people hired O'Neill. He made unfortunate problems go away, the kind of problems that would cause trouble for important people.

Jones grunted and gestured ahead with his rifle. "I've picked up more small thermal traces. Whatever trick he has doesn't do anything about his residuals."

O'Neill snickered and looked at one of the wizards. "With all those fancy spells, it comes down to good old technology in the end. This is why magic won't amount to shit overall. Tech merely needs to get moving again."

The wizard shrugged, disinterest on his face. "We can use similar spells anytime you want, O'Neill."

"Save that shit. I'm only busting your balls."

He had worked with both wizards before, and they were good when it came time to hurt people. It was rewarding to partner with people who weren't squeamish but also weren't overly fond of killing. Sadists made poor business partners. Sometimes, you needed to kill extra people, but at other times, you didn't. Self-control was important in his line of work.

The leader lowered his own AR goggles into place and tapped the side. Faint residual red-yellow thermal tracks of a humanoid appeared before him. He tapped again to return to normal vision and frowned. Something didn't sit right with him, but he couldn't quite grasp what it was. At least they were close and could finish the job soon.

"Usually, when they throw the kinds of bonuses we're getting around, you have to bring the bastard back," he muttered. "Remember that the thing in Vienna, Jones? It's been two years, and I'm still pissed."

The other mercenary laughed. "Things went fine until that damned bastard with all the fancy gadgets and that elf bitch showed up. With shit like that, he had to be some government asshole, and I keep thinking about how it was the US government who hired us to grab that kid, to begin with. The fucking left hand doesn't know what the right hand is doing."

O'Neill nodded. "The middlemen always think we don't know what is going on."

One of the wizards chuckled.

"You wouldn't have liked it if you almost died and didn't get the rest of your pay." He glared at the man.

Jones nodded. "I still wonder what all that was about.

As far as I can tell, the kid wasn't a magical, so I don't know why they needed major firepower to pick him up originally. And who the hell was he, anyway?"

He shook his head. "I don't know and I don't care. Maybe the client knew the gadget bastard and the elf bitch would show up. Like I said, I'm still angry about it. Sometimes, I think about looking around for Light Elves named Daisy. I heard the guy with her say that name before they escaped with the kid."

"What's the point? That's probably not her real name. She's an elf, right? That was probably only a code name. Damn. She was hot, too."

A wizard snickered.

Jones shrugged. "She was. And she wore this tight-ass outfit. It was distracting."

O'Neill snorted. "I don't care about how hot some bitch is once she screws me out of a payday, but that's the thing. There's no profit in going after Daisy and gadget boy, but maybe we'll get lucky someday and get a job to take them out." He frowned. "I wonder if this is more government left-hand-right-hand shit. I'd almost pay them if we end up able to kill gadget boy and the elf."

"You think it is some government shit?" Jones looked at the ground and then at his team leader.

"Probably. You heard the briefing. The target has a host of fancy technomagic implants. Even if it's some company messing around with it, you know they're doing it for the government. It's not like they can get away with that kind of stuff otherwise." He shrugged. "I bet that's how all this shit will go down in the future—magic cyborgs."

One of the wizards hissed his disapproval.

O'Neill grinned at him. "Does it offend your delicate magical sensibilities to know it won't be all your wand shit? People won't need all that hocus pocus. You'd better save your money because you'll be out of a job."

"Magic will still be necessary to create the magical cyborg, O'Neill," the wizard retorted. "And it'll be far more dynamic than any device."

"I'm sure they'll figure that shit out, too. It's a matter of time. Don't bet against the future. You'll always win."

Jones threw a fist up and raised his gun. Everyone froze for a moment, then raised their own weapons and wands and swept the area for the target. O'Neill's heart rate kicked up, and he slowed his breathing. It was time to earn some easy money.

"The tracks suddenly end," the other man whispered. He looked around the area. "I see a few animals here and there, but nothing else. No hint of the project." He tapped the side of his AR goggles.

The team leader frowned and looked around, his jaw tight. "Wait a second." He raised his head slowly. A tree branch was cracked. He flipped the safety off and crept toward the tree, his gun at the ready.

One of the wizards chanted a spell. The footprints leading to the trunk and a single glowing handprint appeared.

"So he's definitely here," O'Neill muttered and backed away from the tree. "Hey, we know you're here," he shouted. "The only chance you have to survive this thing is to come out right away and surrender. If I have to chase you everywhere, I'll be damned pissed about it, and I can't be sure what I'll do."

Jones glanced at him and the leader shook his head. If they could lie to the target and coax him into the line of fire, that was all they needed. The guy was allegedly brainwashed with some sort of near robotic-like personality anyway. It wouldn't be that hard to trick him.

Both wizards raised their wands and cast shield spells. Shimmering light surrounded them.

"Hey, I'm only paid to find you and bring you back, pal," the merc continued. "If you want to blow up some assholes again after I deliver you, that's fine. It's not my problem. So why don't you make this nice and easy and come out? Because you can't escape thanks to the tracking implant you have in you."

The wizards spun and one screamed, "Behind us."

O'Neill didn't even look. Instead, he immediately raced for cover behind a thick trunk and Jones did the same. Surviving an ambush was, first and foremost, about not being an easy target during the chaos of the initial attack.

Their quarry blurred into sight five yards away and his naked form exposed all the glyphs and silver-gold implants in his body. His right hand was surrounded by a red-orange nimbus of light. Light stubble covered his head.

The team leader marveled for a second at the man's ability to wander around without clothes when it was so wet and chilly. The man launched into an attack and snapped the mercenary's attention back to the moment. He aimed his rifle, but the damned wizards were in the line of fire.

The first man pointed his wand and quickly uttered a spell. A thick metal chain appeared and careened toward the charging man. He simply ducked the restraint by bending so far backward that O'Neill had to question if he still possessed a rigid spine.

The other wizard pointed his wand at the ground, but he had no time to utter his spell before the target closed on him. The naked man shoved his energy-covered hand forward. It flashed and cut through the man's shield to claw into his chest.

A harsh scream ripped from the man's throat, and the scent of charred flesh filled the air.

Their adversary's hand passed completely through his body. He yanked it out, and the wizard fell to his knees, where he teetered and managed a low groan before dying.

The surviving wizard pointed his wand at his feet. A loud crack sounded, and he catapulted back several yards, propelled by a sudden burst of air magic.

A red-orange bolt erupted from their quarry's hand and exploded against the wizard. The magical's shield flashed, and he grimaced as he splashed into a muddy puddle.

The man launched another two quick bolts. The second made it through and left a burning hole in the center of the man's coat and shirt along with charred flesh.

The wand spun free and splashed into a puddle nearby. He crawled frantically to reach it.

O'Neill darted from around the tree and fired a burst of anti-magic rounds into the broad chest. The man stumbled before he launched a bolt toward his attacker. The missile slammed home and the energy dissipated around him. His anti-magic deflector darkened.

The mercenary grinned. "It looks like your trick isn't so useful now, is it? I can take your primary attack, but can you take mine?" His smile faded when he saw the bullet wounds begin to close. "Screw it. There's more where that came from."

He fired again and the target jerked, but his expression remained cold and impassive.

The man stared at O'Neill as he flung another energy bolt into the wizard as the man reached for his wand. The resulting explosion left a sizzling, half-burned corpse in the mud.

Both non-magicals fired as their opponent sprinted toward two trees that grew close together. They clipped him despite his inhuman speed before he disappeared behind a trunk. Blood splattered the ground, and the color stood out against the dark and muddy forest floor.

The mercenaries crept forward and followed the trail of blood. They both took position on either side of the tree concealing their quarry before they spun around it, ready to shoot.

No one awaited the men and there was no trace of any blood either.

O'Neill jerked his rifle around in search of the target. "Where the hell did he go?"

Branches rustled above them, and he raised his rifle. He fired off a burst that narrowly missed the man. The tech-nomagic monstrosity dropped to land behind Jones.

He extended his hands and snapped the merc's neck in one fluid movement. The mercenary didn't even manage a yelp of surprise before his body collapsed.

The killer grabbed the corpse and held it up with one arm. He snatched the man's fallen rifle with the other.

"You son of a bitch," O'Neill screamed.

The monstrosity hurled the dead man toward his teammate without even the decency of a grunt of strain. The mercenary jumped aside to avoid the huge corpse, which splashed into the damp beside him and splattered him with mud.

O'Neill turned to open fire, but the target already waited with the rifle in hand and pulled the trigger. Several bullets drove the mercenary back. Pain blossomed through his chest, and he gritted his teeth. His bulletproof vest had saved his life, but not his ribs. He landed hard with a grunt of pain.

Without sitting up, he ripped a sonic grenade from his belt and threw it toward his adversary. A high-pitched whine filled the air, but the man didn't react at all. Instead, he aimed the rifle casually and fired into the mercenary's exposed arm. O'Neill cried out in pain and dropped his weapon.

The target marched toward him. "Their mistake was in thinking the programming would hold. Thank you for the clothes, the deflector, and the intelligence about the beacon. I wasn't sure if it still worked." His hand glowed again as he thrust into his own chest to rake out a small metal disc. With a flare of his hand, it vaporized.

The merc sucked in slow breaths, but each helped to suffuse pain throughout his body. "I don't know your deal, but you're a fucking twisted mistake."

In response, he placed the rifle to O'Neill's head. "I agree with that, but now, everyone will pay for this mistake." He pulled the trigger.

CHAPTER EIGHTEEN

Alison offered a pleasant smile to the frowning Helen as she stepped into the PDA field office. The receptionist harrumphed and nodded toward Agent Latherby's open office door. After all these months, the woman still harbored resentment toward Alison despite her role in helping ferret out the mole in the local PDA.

You can't win everyone over, I suppose.

Helen's boss, Agent Latherby, had called her that morning and requested she come as soon as possible. She'd long since learned that such requests were not made lightly.

I hope some dark wizard moles haven't slipped in again. I thought I could cruise to Christmas without any trouble, but it looks like the PDA has one last adventure for the year. Merry Christmas.

She headed into the office and closed the door behind her. "Will she ever like me, Agent Latherby?" She gestured with her thumb over her shoulder in Helen's general direction.

The shaven-headed agent motioned to the seat in front of his desk. "It's unlikely, at this point. But don't concern yourself with it. Thank you for coming to see me on such short notice, Miss Brownstone. I know you've been busy of late, and I apologize for having to call you in so abruptly. Unfortunately, I became aware of a dangerous situation that necessitates your unique combination of skills and dedication. If I had suspected the situation might arise at all or was aware of it ahead of time, I could have taken other measures to manage it."

Alison waved a hand and took a seat. "Don't worry about it. I know you won't call me without good reason. But please tell me it's not dark wizards. Because if it is, it means they haven't gotten the message, and we'll have to start moving up the Brownstone Harriken Scale of Punishment. That's not really something I want to make a New Year's Resolution." She sighed.

Agent Latherby offered her a thin smile. "Let me offer you this, then, as a small holiday gift. This situation has nothing to do with dark wizards, but that's perhaps the only positive thing I can say about it. Other than that, for various reasons, it's unlikely that your involvement will result in any lasting enemies such as your various dealings with the dark wizards."

"Oh, good. The number of powerful people who roughly fall into the general category of my enemies has increased by more than you would expect lately." She frowned, alerted by the seriousness in his expression. "What's up, then? I expect this goes far beyond artifact smuggling by some gang if you've called me and not simply sent in a government team."

"First of all, this isn't a Seattle matter," he replied. "There is an off-the-books situation that I need your help with—very off-the-books. I won't waste time with much preamble to explain how I came across the information I'm about to relate. It's only important to note that I have found out through my own channels that a very dangerous man escaped from a private research facility located in southwest Washington. The facility was destroyed and all personnel were killed during the escape, partially because of the abilities this man has. We have every reason to believe he'll ruthlessly kill anyone he encounters."

"Hold on. I don't understand a few things." She frowned. "He 'escaped' from a private research facility? Why would someone need to escape from a research facility? Is it a research facility or a prison?"

"Why indeed would someone need to escape from such a place?" Agent Latherby steepled his fingers. "That links into some other things I've learned, such as the fact that a large amount of government money went toward supporting this facility. Billions of dollars."

Alison's frown deepened to a scowl. "That's a lot of money for a private research facility."

"Indeed. I don't know all the details, but what little I have uncovered suggests this is some sort of black-ops experimental operation. It is the kind of thing that would never get congressional approval for funding, which means whoever is funding it is playing more than a few tricks to divert money to the project. Or, at least, they were until recently. I would assume, after this fiasco, that this particular project will be terminated."

"I'm sure the government has tons of secret projects

like that." She shrugged. "It's not like they always admit everything they're working on."

"True, but most don't involve generating a dangerous monster, and all indications suggest the point of the project was to do something exactly like that."

She grimaced. "That's...unfortunate. Why would someone approve something like this? Even if it worked out without an escape, wouldn't they eventually have to explain to the public why they made something like this?"

"Exactly." He nodded. "But unfortunately, there's always someone in the government somewhere who thinks they have to push the envelope for the good of the country. I won't insult you by pretending I never do something questionable based on a regulations standpoint. That's not my criticism. My issue is that these actions have endangered American lives, and it should be the primary concern of everyone in the government—especially if they are in law enforcement or the military to focus on the protection of American lives. Anything that fails at that fails at the fundamental purpose of a government."

He shook his head, his disapproval patent. "It was bad enough before the gates opened, but now, many of those same paranoid people are convinced there will be some sort of monster or magic gap. This, in turn, leads to particularly foolish efforts such as twisted experiments or research into strategic-level magic that we've signed treaties not to use. This country has enough enemies without adding the Oricerans to the list."

Alison tilted her head as she absorbed all the information. She wasn't sure if she would have preferred some dark wizards to beat up over being involved in some multilayered combination of government bureaucratic screwup and conspiracy.

"What and who is this escaped man exactly?" she asked finally. "If he's killing people and helping destroy facilities, he's not someone who is really good at playing the trumpet."

"If only, Miss Brownstone. As far as I can tell, the escaped prisoner is a technomagic modified soldier of unknown origin." Agent Latherby wrinkled his nose in disgust. "I've heard this might be called Project Revenant, and the implications in the name itself are beyond disturbing. I pray that it's only a name and doesn't represent something more unsettling and necromantic, but I also can't ignore the possibility that such a situation is the case."

She winced and recalled how many messed-up things she'd heard in her time from both her mother and father. Given what she witnessed with Scott Carlyle, she wasn't actually surprised that the government might experiment with magical super-soldiers—including potentially dead ones.

I don't agree with Rasila that everyone's obsessed with power, but there are enough people who are to make things bad for everyone else. This is the government's mistake.

Alison sighed and folded her arms. "Look, it sounds messed up, but I'm not so sure I'm the one who should handle something like this, and it's not clear to me why I should, either. You're the PDA. Why don't your people handle it? I'm not trying to be a bitch, but let's say I'm tired of spending this December taking care of problems caused by people's arrogant disregard for others."

He shook his head. "I wish I could personally lead a

team to deal with this situation, but the problem is I can only bend the rules that restrain me to a limited degree, whereas you answer to no one, not even a boss. I'm a creature of the government, and right now, I'm on a leash."

"How?"

"Well, it's obvious that many important people are running scared and trying to conceal their involvement in this project. That includes not authorizing the necessary assets to eliminate this revenant, or whatever you want to call him." His mouth twitched, evidence of his frustration. "In fact, the PDA has been explicitly not authorized to go after the escaped prisoner on the grounds that it's an 'internal DoD matter' for the moment, and they will resolve it."

Alison lowered her arms. "Doesn't that mean the military will be brought in, then?"

"For them to actually deal with it would require spending resources, and they haven't activated any military or other DoD assets to neutralize this...thing or moved any toward it. This is what annoys me so much, Miss Brownstone." Agent Latherby took a deep breath. "Right now, a dangerous pseudo-magical is on the loose, and all anyone is doing is keeping a rough eye on him. They act like it's more important that their involvement not get out than it is to eliminate the target. I wouldn't be even half-surprised if they treat the whole thing as a field test. That might explain the feebleness of their last effort."

"That's a lot of conspiracies to worry about, Agent Latherby."

He stared at her with a piercing look. "You were the victim of a billionaire's magiobiological research. Dark wizards laid a complicated web to destroy you and capture your friend."

She held a hand up. "Okay, okay, I get it. Sometimes, it's not paranoia if they are actually out to get you and all that. Are you saying they haven't tried to stop this thing at all, then?" Could one even call it a man?

"No, that's inaccurate. They did deploy a team of four mercenaries to engage the revenant. He defeated them with ease, and I can't find any indication that they've sent anyone else. The project, as they call him, was originally in a research center several miles outside of La Center in Clark County. They've played it off as an industrial accident, and the locals have accepted the story." Agent Latherby frowned. "Prior to their deaths, the recovery team tracked the escapee to forests in Cowlitz County, but we're not completely sure where. We can only get a general idea of where he is going."

Alison nodded. "So, he's not moving super-fast. He's still in southwest Washington, but I don't understand why no one's completely sure. Can't you use some tracking spells? If he's not teleporting or portaling, he should be easy to eliminate, even without a handicap."

"If only. This subject has the ability to fade from sight and various implants and wards that help to suppress his magical signature from afar. He had a purely technological tracking beacon in him before, but he's since removed it after the last encounter, which makes his movements more elusive." He leaned back in his chair, his expression grim. "As the target is in a rural part of the county, we still do have a window of opportunity to stop him without involving the general public. We have indirect evidence that suggests he's traveling northeast, so we also have an idea where we could intercept him as well."

"Wait, so you have an experiment that is probably a government experiment. Not only that, they don't want to admit it's a problem and handle it like they should right away. And you basically want me to go in unofficially with my team to eliminate a dangerous technomagic monster?" Alison raised an eyebrow in challenge. "I don't know if I like the sound of that."

"Yes, Miss Brownstone," Agent Latherby replied, his tone flat. "I would say that's a very accurate summary of this particular situation. In other circumstances, I wouldn't be so quick to bring you in, especially because of some of the political implications, but we're depending on luck more than strategy right now to save innocent people's lives."

"What do you mean?"

Alison found it difficult to muster sympathy for dead mercenaries and twisted researchers, but the idea of innocent people dying at the hands of some monster created by a black project funded by the government tightened her stomach.

"On his current trajectory, he will initially encounter no real threats. We can't account for every stray person in a cabin, but in general, people should be safe for the initial part of his journey." He retrieved his phone and brought up a map of western Washington and tapped Mt. St. Helens in the southwest. "But the escapee is on an intercept path with the mountain, and there is significant tourist activity around there. If we want to stop him, we need to strike before he arrives. Otherwise, innocent people will assuredly die."

She stared at the map and recalled the mountain from her earlier flyby. "And you're sure the government won't clean the mess up? As in sending in Marines, not disposable mercenaries."

The PDA agent shook his head. "Not until it's too late. I think the mercenaries are the maximum level of effort they're willing to invest until their hand is forced."

"But they have to care that it might kill people. More people."

"I would make no such assumption. I've been around long enough and fought enough turf wars to recognize something very dirty when I encounter it. I'm sure this entire incident will eventually end with some sort of congressional investigation, but I don't care about that. I also don't care about everyone participating in the rush to protect themselves. They've lost control of this project, and we can't allow innocent citizens to suffer." His voice rose toward the end. "That's why I need you, Miss Brownstone."

"Are you okay?" Alison eyed him with suspicion. He wasn't acting like the calm and collected agent she was used to dealing with. "You seem a little on edge."

"I apologize if I've made you uncomfortable," he replied in a quieter, more controlled voice. "This has brought up some bad memories. It's unprofessional of me to let them affect my briefing."

"Bad memories? That's the theme of my life these past few weeks. What happened?"

Agent Latherby cleared his throat. "Earlier in my career, I was involved in a similar incident where the government didn't move fast enough. Far too many inno-cent people were hurt because too many officials were more concerned about keeping their jobs than doing what was necessary to protect American lives. I vowed then that if I was ever involved in a similar situation, I would do everything I could to facilitate its quick resolution." He raised his chin and squared his shoulders. "And fortunately, I have you as an asset. Please note I'm not asking you to do this for free. I have certain discretionary funds I can use."

"If this is about assholes covering for themselves, won't the rest of the government be pissed that some random security contractor has stuck her nose in their business?"

"Perhaps, but I have a few contacts and favors I can use to ameliorate that issue." Agent Latherby scoffed quietly. "Once I help facilitate people learning of your involvement, the government would be even less likely to get involved. If this isn't a simple field test, they should be happy to let you deal with it, and they have no reason to anger you. Many people are aware of how your father feels about govern-ment harassment of your family."

"Fine. I'll do it." Alison frowned and shook her head. "But I should have known."

"Known?"

"It's only that I'm cleaning up many people's mistakes this month." She stood and tugged her jacket down. "But it's like you said. Innocent people shouldn't have to pay for other people's mistakes."

He nodded, gratitude in his eyes. "I'll send you what little I know about the escapee."

CHAPTER NINETEEN

With Mason at the wheel, the SUV rumbled over the ground and kicked up mud to splatter the sides of the vehicle. The four-wheel drive enabled the team to travel off-road in the forest without too much trouble, but the increasing density of the trees continued to threaten their efforts. Alison could easily fly, but she didn't intend to leave Mason, Hana, and Drysi behind.

I have a team, and I should use them. They know what they're doing. Izzie and I wouldn't have been able to pull Vancouver off without them.

Fortunately, the remnants of a few old logging roads helped them move closer to the target area without too much trouble or needing magic to pull a stuck vehicle out of the mud. They had already driven to the last known sighting of the revenant and now proceeded in a generally northeastern direction. There were no obvious signs or tracks thus far.

"I still think we should have taken the helicopter," Hana

complained. "Rather than driving around in an SUV half-sinking into the mud in the middle of the forest."

Alison shook her head, her gaze fixed on Mt. St. Helens looming in the distance. "From what Latherby told me, the guy can fire explosive bolts, and a helicopter's too tempting a target. To fly around with us shielding it would tire us out too quickly. It's fine. Our guy was close enough to Seattle that we didn't have to spend a whole day driving to get here or anything, and we have aerial visibility covered already. Tahir, do you see anything?"

Their drones were deployed in a loose net over a much wider area. It took all of Tahir and Sonya's efforts and automated algorithms to keep up with the drones and possible hits while also ensuring they didn't crash.

"Alas, no," the infomancer responded through her receiver. "Sonya and I will keep our drone swarm, as it were, in the air, but from what you've told us, if this revenant's concealment abilities also extend into the infrared, we might have little ability to spot him anyway. The thickness of the trees also complicates matters. Sonya and I can control individual drones and fly them easily through the forest, but the whole group is a different matter. We have to keep most of the drones much higher, which only makes it even harder to spot a potential single humanoid in the woods from above."

"Okay, do your best," she replied. "At least it's not raining. Agent Latherby will also call me if he comes across any information on sightings. I don't know if the government has anything useful now that they've lost the tracking beacon, but at least it's another source of information. We might get lucky."

"Lucky?" Mason shook his head and frowned. He kept both hands on the wheel. They couldn't race through the forest without risking collision, but as far as they knew, the enemy didn't have any superior mobility in that he wasn't too far from the original lab despite having days to travel. Even driving slowly gave them an advantage and a chance to catch up. "I wouldn't count on luck."

Alison shrugged. "I'm not counting on luck, but I also won't push it away if it wants to help us out. I'll take whatever I get. I'd take Raven's help right now if she wanted to offer it."

"I merely think we need to be realistic about this," he suggested.

"And what does being realistic mean in this situation?" She raised a white eyebrow.

"We have to ask ourselves if we will even be able to find this guy under these conditions. Like you said, at least it's not raining, but the last team had a tracking signal, whereas we're simply driving through the forest and hoping we can find a single man who can literally turn invisible." His expression darkened. "I'm not convinced we can find him, at least not in any sort of timely manner."

"We can try. That's the only option. Without anything personal, we can't do better than what we tried at the office. If none of us can execute a basic tracking spell against the target, that suggests he has decent magical anti-tracking defenses, which is consistent with what I was told. Since the government's tried to pretend this isn't happening, it's not like they will provide us with anything for a directional tracking spell, and since they didn't try one earlier, it means it wouldn't even work."

His frown deepened and he shook his head.

"If you have something else to say, then spit it out, Mason," Alison suggested. She wasn't irritated that he had problems with the job, but she didn't want him to wall himself off.

"I'm simply not fond of the job." Mason shook his head. "Not fond of it at all. And not because I think it'll be a pain in the ass. We've had plenty of pain in the ass jobs before."

"Then what's bothering you about it?"

"Because it's cleaning up a government mess." He snorted. "We're not some black-ops janitors, but even Latherby is treating us that way. I don't like it. It's a lot of risk for something they'll simply deny later."

"How is that any different than cleaning up Raven's mess?" She tried to keep an accusatory tone of out her voice. "Her mess wasn't her trying to protect the county or make the world a better place. She simply messed something up and screwed up badly when she created something terrible."

Hana and Drysi leaned forward, both with curious expressions.

Don't get too excited. This isn't about me being jealous of Raven.

Alison was actually rather surprised by how little she cared about Mason's previous relationship. He had been given multiple opportunities to return to Raven before and after meeting Alison, and he always chose not to, which meant he didn't love the woman. That was all she needed to know.

Mason chuckled, but there was no mirth in it. "I wasn't all that fond of that job either. I made that clear from the beginning, and it wasn't only because of my personal feelings about Raven, but there's still a key difference."

"Oh?" She folded her arms. "Please elaborate."

"Raven's a messed-up witch with very few people around who are willing to tell her not to do something inappropriate and immoral. The only people's she's around these days are the opposite. But the government should at least be a little smarter about this kind of crap, even if we are talking about some secret military black-ops project. Seriously, 'Don't be as bad as the sociopathic witch' is a damned low bar to clear, and whoever is responsible for this Project Revenant failed even that. The idea that they might end up getting out of this without any repercussions pisses me off."

"I doubt that'll happen," she replied. "Especially if certain people like Agent Latherby push from their end. He's as angry as you are about this." She sighed and slumped against her seat. "And it's always important to remember we have people like Agent Latherby trying to do the right thing and not merely pulling CYA. I won't say I'm overly trusting of the government considering some of the things people from the government have tried to do to my family through the years, but people like Agent Latherby and Senator Johnston have helped me out. I accept it's not monolithic, and it doesn't change the fact this job is about protecting innocent people and not the government."

Drysi cleared her throat. "I won't lie. I like the job better than our normal sort. A lot more."

Alison glanced into the back seat at the witch. "You do?"

"Yes. Search and destroy is bloody easy." She blew out a long, slow breath. "It's closer to the kind of thing I used to do, but at least, in this case, I'm doing it to help people out rather than helping others take control of them. It's me combining the two main jobs I had in an easy way, and I don't have to go around town talking to informants."

"That makes sense."

Mason nodded. "Yes, it does." He slowed and drove around a felled log. "To make it clear, A, I might not like the job, but I'll do what I need to. I do hope we find this guy before he hurts someone else."

"I understand where you're coming from. Trust me. I've felt it, too." She turned to look out the window at the trees. "I'm also definitely thinking about a New Year's Resolution where I don't help clean up anyone else's messes for a few months."

Especially if I have to concentrate on the Drow mess.

Everyone chuckled, oblivious to her inner concerns.

"There's no reason to brood about the job," Hana pointed out. "We might drive around for a few hours. Let's talk about something more interesting than how hard it is to find strange government project super-soldiers. Let's talk about something happy."

"Such as what?" Alison asked, incredulity in her tone.

"Omni, of course." She relayed the answer as if it was self-evident. Honestly, she talked about the animal with all the obsession of a mother discussing her newborn baby.

She laughed. "Did some suspicious Light Elves say hi to you and now you're convinced King Oriceran's ready to portal in for a pet raid? Are you begging Tahir to set up more wards?"

The infomancer grunted over the line but didn't say anything. Alison suspected he was concentrating too much on the drones to join in—or perhaps he wanted to be spared another conversation about his girlfriend's latest obsession.

The fox snorted. "The whole King Oriceran coming for Omni thing is so yesterday's news, and I realized that if I obsessed over that kind of thing, I was doing what all of you had been doing, and I don't want to do that."

"And what is that exactly?"

"Trying to solve the mystery of Omni." Hana raised her brow and nodded as if she'd offered the most intriguing nugget of wisdom ever to her friends. "So I won't worry until the mystery unravels itself, and I'll concentrate on getting the most out of Omni in the meantime."

Drysi's face pinched in confusion. "And how do you do that with a shapeshifting pet?"

Hana shook a finger. "I'm glad you asked. The first thing I've done is try to catalog all the different animals Omni turns into. There are some repeats, but there are also some major noticeable holes in the line-up in terms of overall types of animals."

"And what are those?"

"Fish and amphibians. He's been a bunch of birds, mammals, and lizards." She mimed a fish swimming and then a frog hopping. "But no fish and no amphibians. I should help him live up to his potential, and that involves him becoming the occasional fish or even a frog."

Alison thought she saw movement in a side mirror, but it was nothing more than a branch swaying in the wind. "By doing what exactly? He probably doesn't turn into a fish because he doesn't want to suffocate if no one's around to put him in water. Same thing for amphibians. There's too much of a risk of him drying out."

A thoughtful expression spread over Hana's face. "I hadn't thought of that, but it's a good possibility. Maybe if I kept him in water more he might change, if not to a fish than an amphibian."

"I don't get this." Alison shook her head. "Aren't you the one who once told me fish are basically only glorified decorations?"

Hana nodded. "They are, basically. You can't really cuddle a fish. What good is a pet you can't cuddle?"

Drysi chuckled. "You're the one who wants your pet to turn into a fish or a bloody frog. Can you cuddle frogs?"

"It's not about that. I merely want to make sure he lives up to his full potential." Hana shrugged. "And it would be neat, which is a good enough reason itself."

The SUV rattled as they passed through a rough patch of terrain. It smoothed out a moment later upon their arrival at an overgrown dirt road. Mason eased up on the gas pedal and pointed. "Sorry to interrupt the Omni Chronicles, but do you see what I see?"

Alison leaned forward. "It looks like tracks. I wonder if our guy got arrogant or if something else went wrong—like a shortage of energy."

"Who knows? But at least it's worth following." He accelerated gently.

She frowned and put a hand on his arm. "Stop the car."

He applied the brakes, and the car rumbled to a stop. "What is it?"

"I'll take to the air. If it is our guy, I might be able to see him first, and I can take an explosive bolt or two—unlike a helicopter." She unfastened her seatbelt and opened the door. "I'll contact you if I see him."

Mason nodded. "Be careful, A. This guy has already killed way too many people."

Shadow wings sprouted from her back. She layered a few shields over herself with more shadow magic than she usually did, which left a less transparent shield than normal. "And I want to make sure he doesn't kill more people."

Alison closed the door and took flight. She elevated for a dozen yards before she moved forward. They were close. Their target had to be somewhere nearby.

CHAPTER TWENTY

Alison soared through the forest and occasionally lowered her altitude when she caught sight of something that might possibly be a man, only to be disappointed at a man-shaped stump or plant. It had been about twenty minutes since she left the vehicle, and the constant energy expenditure to fuel her wings increased the sense of general fatigue that suffused her body. Her aerial reconnaissance through the forest hadn't proved useful at all.

The SUV continued along the original trail, but the tracks disappeared after a few minutes. Other than traveling to the northeast, they currently had no leads. For all they knew, the revenant had already changed direction.

Mason might be right. This might be hopeless. It might be better for Latherby to convince the rest of the government to set up response teams at all the nearest towns. This guy eventually has to come up for air, and they can eliminate them. Either that or they have to give us something personal so we can hopefully try a directional tracking spell.

"I have something," Sonya shouted, the voice almost a

screech through the receiver. The sudden declaration distracted Alison, and she crashed through a few branches with a grunt.

She removed herself from the tangle of branches and flew higher. "You do?" Hope tinged her voice. "Please tell me it's something useful. I'll take a single set of tracks at this point."

"I think I have a whole trail."

"Damn. Really?"

"Yeah. I checked the area again where the tracks disappeared," the girl explained. "I tried to get different viewing angles from different drones and noticed broken branches. I also saw there were branches broken not only in one tree, so I don't think it's storm damage."

"I concur with her assessment," Tahir added.

Alison grinned. "Our guy uses his concealment abilities, but they don't help him keep the tracks from the ground so simple good old-fashioned tree-to-tree movement does the trick."

The infomancer cleared his throat. "We'll converge all the drones to follow the limb path. We now have a good idea where he's been and will be."

Alison's grin faded. Her team was good, but the federal government had access to similar resources, which meant their failure to pinpoint the enemy was more a lack of will than an impossibility. Maybe Latherby was right and they were treating the whole situation as a field test.

"That sounds good," she replied. "It's time to find him in the flesh. Mason, go ahead and stop. I'll fly back to you, and we'll let our drone swarm track our target, and we'll take him on together."

"Good. See you soon, A."

"See you soon." She turned toward the overgrown road and the SUV in the distance and sped toward it. "And good job, Sonya. You might have ensured that we can pull this job off."

"T-thanks, Alison," the girl replied. "When you say it, it means a lot."

Now back in the SUV, Alison's heart pounded hard. She had been half-convinced before that Mason was right about their inability to find the man, but they had a good chance at tracking the escapee and ending his rampage before he hurt any more people—or, at least, any innocent people. The revenant might be powerful, but he was still far more limited than a true magical, and that limitation might prove the key to finding and stopping him.

If he could fly, he would probably be halfway across the country by now.

"We have a problem," Tahir explained, irritation in his voice.

"We have many problems with this mission alone," she responded. "What are you talking about in this specific case?"

"I just had positive if brief visual confirmation of the revenant. His invisibility field flickered for a moment. He's spotted at least one of the drones, I suspect, but hasn't engaged them for whatever reason."

Alison glanced at Mason, who looked tenser than before when they were driving. "I don't understand how that's a problem. It's what we wanted from when we started our search. Once we know exactly where he is or at least where he's going, we can corner him and finish this crap."

"That's not the problem," Tahir continued. "I sent drones further out to check along the route. I searched with tactical potential in a battle, and I discovered a group of campers directly in his path. He's almost certain to encounter them on his present route, and I don't have any reason to believe they can defend themselves against Omni, let alone the revenant."

"Don't disrespect my fur-feather-scale baby," Hana complained.

Alison sighed. "Who goes camping in the woods in December in western Washington? Things had to get complicated."

"I've tried to warn them off," the infomancer explained. "Via direct transmissions to their phones, but judging by what they said, they think it's a prank and have shut their phones off."

She scrubbed a hand down her face. "How close are we?"

"Still several minutes out, but they're off the main road. You won't be able to drive directly there. It's only because the revenant has moved further away from the road that he'll intercept them."

"Understood." She grimaced. "Mason, time to let me out again."

Alison cut through the forest using a new shield so she only had to avoid the largest branches. A straight flight brought her quickly to the campsite. No deadly techno-magic revenant was there murdering anyone. That was always a bonus.

Two men and two women in thick jackets and knitted caps stared in confusion as she descended from the sky with her dark wings spread behind her. She landed in front of their large green tent and took a moment to examine the campers. They looked like they were in their early twenties. Their cheeks were red, and their pupils were dilated in bloodshot eyes. The pungent herbal odor of marijuana hung in the air.

Oh, great. This explains why they didn't listen to Tahir.

"You need to leave immediately," Alison ordered.

One of the men stepped forward, his movements unsteady. "Are you supposed to be a fallen angel? Because that's a little on the nose to have dark wings."

"Huh?" She blinked in confusion. "Oh, the wings." She released the energy that fueled them. "No, I'm not a fallen angel, but you need to get out of here now. It's not safe. You didn't listen to my friend, but you have to listen to me before you get hurt."

"What's not safe?" The man shook his head. "Our sleeping bags are good for negative forty degrees, and this tent's sealed tighter than my old apartment." He gestured widely. "Nature is way safer than the city. Did you ever get mugged by a chipmunk?"

"Not yet, but December's not over yet."

He chuckled and shook his fingers at her. "You're

funny." He pointed and looked at his friends. "She's funny, right?"

"Definitely funny," the other man replied.

The two women laughed but didn't say anything.

Alison gestured frantically with her hands. "Alison Brownstone shows up and tells you to get the hell out of somewhere because it's not safe, and you blow it off like it's a joke? I know you're high, but you're not that high."

"Am I supposed to know who you are?" He looked at his friends, and their shrugs and confused expressions suggested they didn't have any more clue than he did. "I'm not much into celebrity news."

"Of all the times..." She gritted her teeth and took a deep breath. "I don't have time to explain other than to say a very dangerous person is coming this way. I think me and my friends can stop him, but you need to get somewhere safe because this might get messy. I don't want to see any of you get hurt, even if you are kind of damned annoying right now."

The camper frowned and pursed his lips. "Oh, I see what this is. I totally see it."

His friends nodded as if they could read his mind.

"You do?" Alison asked. "Then get the hell out of here already."

The man shook his head. "I've read all about how plenty of Oricerans are all really into nature. You have those wings and everything, so I bet you're a dryad. You're not what I expected, but I totally honor your dryad nature." He slapped his chest twice. "I have nothing but mad respect for you, Dryad Brownstone."

"A dryad? Why would you even... I'm not a dryad, and

I'm telling you your damned lives are in danger. If you really want to know, technically, I'm half-Dark Elf and half-human. Now that's resolved, will you please go?"

Maybe I should start throwing a few spells around to scare them off, but I don't want them to hate Oricerans or the Drow.

"You're running out of time, Alison," Tahir reported. "The revenant's still invisible, but we have branch movement on trees close to you. You need to get those people out of there or prepare for an attack."

The camper studied her curiously and shook his head. "No. Not a dryad. That's wrong. I don't even think you're Oriceran. I think you're some freaky eco-obsessed witch chick who is worried about us damaging the forest." He raised his palm. "We solemnly swear not to fuck things up. You should totally dig us because we're, like, getting back in touch with nature. You need more people like us for your wood witch stuff."

"First of all, I'm not a wood witch. Second, you can get back to nature somewhere else or later," Alison snapped. "I simply need you to get out of here until we can deal with the threat. After that, you can camp and commune with all the dryads you want."

He frowned. "Wait. I thought of something else. How do I know you're not trying to steal our cool tent? That's an expensive tent. I can't experience nature if I actually have to, you know, experience nature." He blinked a few times, a suspicious expression on his face.

"Will you please listen to me?" she shouted. "I'm trying to save your life here."

"Man, you're tense." He rolled his eyes. "You need some weed. Does weed even work on witches? Just say no to dust. It's not natural. Don't let them fool you by saying it's natural because of magic. If you can't grow it, you don't smoke it. That's the rule."

What the hell do I do?

A flash of orange-red light out of the corner of her eye and a pulse of energy alerted her. She tackled the man in the same second that an energy bolt careened through the now empty space where he'd stood and struck the tent. It exploded and left a blackened hole filled with a burning pile of fabric and metal.

"Woah!" the camper shouted. "My tent."

The others yelped in surprise and scurried for the trees. Their speaker shook his head and then sprinted after them.

"Our revenant is here," Alison reported for the benefit of her other team members.

"We're on our way, A," Mason responded over the comms. "We only need a few more minutes."

She gritted her teeth and spread a wide shield before she rushed forward. Another bolt exploded against the shield and stung. She wouldn't be able to take many hits without concentrating the barrier more effectively, but she needed to give them enough protection to get clear.

"These people have done nothing to you," she shouted. "They are only a group of campers who are high."

The four crouched low as they continued their retreat.

"The enemies of the United States must be eliminated," the revenant shouted from the trees. He jumped down and stood before her, now clearly visible in bloody and mud-encrusted forest-pattern camouflage fatigues. A rifle was strapped over his shoulder, and several magazines were tucked into pockets in a vest. A few implants and glyphs on his neck remained visible.

It looks like he took someone's clothes.

Alison gestured toward the cowering campers. "These are innocent people simply trying to get back to nature."

The revenant grunted. "It doesn't matter," he retorted, his voice a rough whisper. "I don't have long. I feel it now. The orders are in my soul." He flung another bolt at her. She hissed in pain and concentrated the shielding around her before she added another few layers.

Without warning, she launched a light bolt at the revenant, but he disappeared, and her missile careened to sink into a nearby branch and sear it.

He didn't teleport, he simply moved. But where?

She searched the tree branches quickly. Her adversary appeared a moment later and launched another explosive bolt. It blasted a cloud of mud and water that splattered her shield.

Okay, so he has to appear to shoot, but he can move otherwise. I can work with that pattern.

Another attack struck her from the side, and she spun in time to fling her arm out and land a shadow crescent. The shadow magic tore through several branches but didn't strike her enemy before he disappeared again.

"I know you probably have no idea who I am," Alison called. "So I won't try that, but you have to realize I'm strong. You've hit me and barely hurt me. From what little I know of what has happened, my guess is you're a victim here, so I'll ask you to surrender. If you do, I can promise I'll do everything in my power to help you."

The revenant appeared atop a branch several trees away. "Surrender?"

She nodded. "I don't want to have to kill you if I can avoid it, but I can't let you hurt innocent people even if they are annoying."

He tilted his head in thought as he stared at her. "No surrender. The enemies of the United States must be eliminated." He flung two energy bolts at her and blinded her in the explosion.

Damn it.

CHAPTER TWENTY-ONE

She extended a shadow blade and wings as she needed mobility if she wanted to have a chance against the revenant. Once in the air, she fired two quick blasts toward the last location of the enemy but only succeeding in severing a tree branch.

It doesn't even seem like he has to charge his attacks much, only that he can't hide while he fires. This will get very annoying really quickly.

"Tahir, how are the campers?" Alison asked.

"They are fleeing the forest with impressive speed and endurance," he reported. "They're almost at the dirt road and well clear of any risk of collateral damage."

"Good."

A distant rumble filled the air, and she wondered if a storm was coming. Dark clouds hung in the sky, but the trees blocked her view of the horizon. She wasn't sure if a storm would be a helpful distraction or merely another obstacle in the current fight.

The revenant reappeared and fell toward the ground. A

stream of bright red-orange energy blasted from his feet, incinerated his boots, and propelled him upward. He pointed his left hand down, and another stream appeared. His sleeve burned away.

He can fly now? Or maybe he could always fly and he was saving energy. This makes things...interesting.

"A, we're trying to get to you," Mason reported.

"Okay," she replied and tried to focus on her now aerial foe. "I need to concentrate for a while."

I have to get this guy to surrender. Killing him is simply killing another victim, and I have to get him to see reason.

The revenant circled Alison and his left hand acted as a directional thruster. His right hand was still free to fire explosive bolts at her. Thankfully, his attacks exploded against several trees and merely damaged some but collapsed others.

She hurtled directly toward him, spun aside to avoid a blast, and fired a couple of light bolts, but her foe disappeared again. Her missiles passed through the space where he had been without striking anything.

Last-minute dodge?

Alison jerked her head from one side to the other in search of the man. She wasn't used to fighting other aerial opponents and might need to practice it more in the training room. But first, she needed to deal with the enhanced man hiding from her.

The revenant reappeared. He plummeted toward the ground before he summoned his magical thrust and avoided a crash by mere inches. His energy scorched the undergrowth, and if it hadn't been so wet, there might have been a risk of a forest fire.

No fear marred his expression.

She took her opportunity to fling a shadow crescent and then a light bolt and only narrowly missed her target. His rapid movements with his hand let him roll and bank with surprising agility. He replied with another attack, but the shot went wide and flew into the sky.

Should I close with a shadow blade?

Another enemy volley forced the thought out of her head.

The pair continued to exchange shots, but the explosive nature of the revenant's attacks blinded her more than once as he blasted limbs and bark all around her. He zoomed between close trees and looped to attack, blasting quicker but weaker bolts at her as she followed. A few struck her and she hissed in pain before she forced more energy into her shields. Despite her efforts, she couldn't land a solid hit.

This guy hits a lot harder than I'm used to.

After an extended exchange of fire with neither side achieving a solid strike, Alison made no effort to dodge the revenant's latest attack and instead, careened directly toward him. The bolts pelted her and quickly whittled her shield down. Pain spread from a burn on her shoulder. Her jacket and shirt both now had a charred hole.

She flung a light bolt at the last moment, which connected with the man's chest. Immediately, she dropped and shoved more energy into restoring her shields.

It's like his attacks are anti-magic the way they ripped my shields down. I have to be careful.

Her adversary tumbled, his shirt burned away and blackened, charred flesh bared beneath. He landed hard and splashed in a shallow puddle but hastily pushed to his feet. The burned flesh sloughed away, and new skin spread slowly over the wounds. The huge hole revealed more glyphs and silver-gold implants on his chest.

Damn, that's fast regeneration. It'll to take a little more than I thought to convince him he can't win, but maybe there's another way.

Alison took several deep breaths and ignored the pain in her shoulder. The glyphs and implants on display only reinforced the pathetic true nature of the man before her. Anger coursed through her—not at the man but at the people who would use magic to warp a living being in such a twisted manner.

"You have to understand, I don't want to hurt you," she shouted. "The government wants this cleaned up, but I only wanted to make sure you didn't hurt anyone. You have to give up. It's obvious to me now that they've messed your mind up, but you're not mindless, and I swear to you that I can find someone to help you. I have powerful friends in the magical community. I know people in the PDA and the government who will help find the people who did this to you and punish them, too, but you have to work with me."

The revenant stared at her. His hands crackled with energy and his eye twitched. "I'm trying to hold onto myself, but I can't." His breathing turned ragged. "It's so hard to concentrate and maintain that. It's like I've been asleep the entire time and I've woken up, but there's someone else in my body and I'm supposed to go back to sleep."

"I can help you." Alison smiled gently and released her

shadow blade. "That's what I do. I didn't fully understand what the situation was before with you, but I do now. All you have to do is stop attacking me. My friends and I could maybe put some kind of binding spell around you. Then, I can take you to get help."

Correk must have some spells that could help him, or he must know someone. With the dark wizard problem taken care of, he doesn't have to be as guarded.

"Damn it, A," Mason called over the comms. "Where are you? You shouldn't be fighting that guy yourself."

She glanced around her and whispered, "Uh, somewhere else. He started flying, and I chased him, but I think I'm getting through to him."

"She's about a half-mile in your current direction," Tahir explained. "I'll switch to direct transmission to you to help guide you and not distract Alison."

"The enemies of the United States must be eliminated," the revenant called. "Magical terrorists must be eliminated."

"I heard you before. You're not some mindless machine. You can fight this. You were a man. No, you are a man." She shook her head. "Try to remember who you were before they changed you. Remember what's truly important."

"I...had..." He groaned and fell to his knees. He put his hands to his head and screamed. "No, I can't. I can't hold onto myself. I don't want to go back to sleep."

"You can fight it, damn it!" she shouted. "If my dad could fight the more advanced version, you can fight this. You are a man, not a machine. Now prove it."

"Alison, what the hell is going on there?" Mason asked. "What does your dad have to do with this?"

"Not now, Mason," she snapped. "Just concentrate on getting to me."

The revenant lowered his arms, his gaze fixed on her. "The enemies of the United States must be eliminated," he intoned, all hint of his personality gone. "Magical terrorists must be eliminated." His eyes twitched, and his mouth curled in a snarl. "I can serve the country by defending it. You are an enemy of the United States. You must be eliminated. The enemies of the United States must be eliminated."

Alison shook her head. "I'm Alison Brownstone. I'm a security contractor. I protect people—like I think you wanted to, but they changed you into this machine. You don't have to be a machine. You're still a man. You still have a soul. Fight it. Remember your past. Remember the happy moments that gave you joy. Remember the sad moments that crushed your soul but remember what it was to be human. Don't let these bastards win."

The rumble grew closer.

Alison's stomach knotted as pity overwhelmed her. Whatever happened there, she didn't want to have to kill the man.

This is what Dad could have become if the situation was slightly different for him. Something like this with Whispy in command. Alive, but not really alive. Damn the people who did this to this man. I'll contact Johnston when this is all done. Some heads better roll over this shit.

"I'm sorry for the distraction, but there's additional trouble," Tahir reported.

"Trouble?" she whispered, her attention still focused on

the man who jerked and twitched occasionally. "What now? Make it quick. I think I've got through to him."

The revenant continued to watch her, uncertainty on his face.

If he's not attacking, I still have a chance.

"Two incoming dropships," Tahir explained.

That would explain the rumble.

"Dropships?" she asked. "Do we have any ID? Military? AET?" She tried to think of any cities nearby that might even be able to field an AET team. They could have flown from a bigger city, but it wouldn't have made sense for them to get there so quickly after the fight had started.

Unless they already knew where the revenant was, or someone was watching us and waiting.

"I...you...can't..." Tahir's voice disappeared under a curtain of static.

What the hell?

The team receivers weren't normal communication gear. They relied partially on Tahir's magic, which meant whoever had jammed the signal also used at least some magic and understood the necessity of it.

I guess you were wrong about people staying out of this, Latherby. I don't blame you, though. You wanted to do what I did —protect people. We'll get the bastards who were responsible for this later. I only need to keep the situation under control for now.

Alison held her hands up in a placating manner. "You need to stop attacking me. I think whoever is responsible for what happened to you is coming soon. If you keep control, I can help hide you while we figure out a way to help you. If they made you into what you are partially with magic, then magic can help undo it. You won't suffer as a machine. I promise you that I can help you."

His eye twitched a few times "The enemies of the United States must be eliminated. Magical terrorists must be eliminated." He raised his hands and blasted two bolts at her. She flew out of the way and the blast blew a huge chunk out of a nearby Douglas fir. A huge crack reverberated around her, and the tree crashed to the ground.

Damn it. This is not the fight I wanted to have.

The energy brightened around the man's hands and lines of energy began to flow all around his body. "Magical terrorists must be eliminated."

I have to take this more seriously. Maybe I can knock him out somehow if I can't convince him to surrender, or at least I can keep him down until we can get him under control. If we stuck him in the containment cell, maybe that would work. Latherby has to have some anti-magic deflectors sitting around. Or we could use a binding spell. There has to be enough power between me, Mason, and Drysi.

She lifted off the ground with the help of her wings, circled the man, and channeled energy into an explosive orb. "I'm sorry. I didn't want to have to do this, but I think I have to knock some sense into you before I can help you."

He followed her progress with his eyes but made no effort to fly as the flow of energy increased around him.

The rumble became a roar which demanded her attention. She looked up.

Two dropships zoomed overhead, their back cargo doors open. Three figures in black armor with thrust packs leapt from the back of each dropship. The six aimed their weapons at Alison and the revenant.

Out of time.

The revenant threw his arms up and released a massive blast of crimson energy into the sky. The attack struck the side of one of the retreating dropships to blow the side engine and wing off. The vehicle spiraled to the ground, a trail of smoke behind it.

Railguns, heavy machine guns, and rockets rained from above. Alison jerked to the side and lost her concentration as the volley blew a crater in the ground. Her orb flew away from her hand and struck a tree to obliterate the central portion and drop the top into the forest with another echoing crash.

A fiery explosion marked the dropship's impact in the distance.

She stayed on the move as the power armored team thrust every few seconds to slow their descent.

A three-way battle. Perfect.

CHAPTER TWENTY-TWO

The revenant lay on the ground, burns and bloody wounds all over his body. New flesh began to form and several of the implants shifted position. A normal man would have been incinerated confetti after such a beating. Alison wasn't sure how well she could have survived such a concentrated attack.

All that damage, but he's still healing.

She stayed close to a tree trunk as she ascended. The newcomers descended slowly, and their thrust packs roared.

After a few seconds, they opened fire on her. She dodged several shots, but a railgun round and an exploding rocket strained her shield. The force smacked her against the tree, dazed. She allowed herself to drop and recharged her shields as a stream of bullets ripped from a machine gun and blew apart the trunk where she had been. Bark and dust rained down on her.

Light cuts and burns covered her body, but she pushed the pain to the edge of her thoughts. It would have to wait until the battle was over. Six adversaries with anti-magic deflectors and heavy weapons was a challenge even for her, especially when she had to potentially worry about the out of control revenant.

He's still healing, so I'll concentrate on them.

Alison thrust her hand out to launch a light bolt and fired several in a row. The nearest attacker absorbed the missiles, thanks to the anti-magic deflector embedded directly in the armor.

The crystal darkened, but it would take concentrated fire if she wanted to shatter it and be able to disable the armor or kill the operator.

Quick flight and layered shields saved her from the river of bullets, railgun rounds, and rockets launched at her. The aggressors were better at hitting a man on the ground than they were a woman flying around. She could win.

Encouraged, she extended two shadow blades and twirled as she charged one of the railgunners who was recharging his weapon. She wound her legs around his torso and hacked at the armor with both blades and rapid blows. The deflector darkened with each attack. The operator slammed the armored fist into her, but her shield absorbed the blow and he accomplished nothing more than a minor sting.

The deflector changed from cloudy to completely dark. Her relentless assault ended with the defense shattered. She took her opportunity and stabbed both blades through the center of his chest. They emerged out the back and confirmed that she'd struck the enemy inside before she pushed off.

For all the advanced technology on display, it was merely a can without a living operator. The thrust pack cut out and the armor plummeted to the ground.

Distracted by Alison, the others didn't notice the half-healed revenant rise and charge a new attack, his entire body again saturated with cascading energy.

I thought he'd be down for the count for longer than that.

Alison flew away from the armored assailants and pushed more energy into her shields and wings and ignored her weapons for the moment.

The revenant released his attack, and the enemy disengaged their thrust packs in a feeble attempt to dodge the energy. The blast exploded around one of them, shattering the deflector in an instant, and blew it and the man inside into burning pieces. A second teammate nearby fared better but lost his deflector.

Alison used her new opportunity to whirl and fly toward the now vulnerable enemy. She readied the two blades and sliced the armored man in half with a sweeping motion.

The three remaining adversaries hesitated for a moment before they turned their weapons on the revenant.

Yeah, in this case, I agree with you.

The railguns and machine guns ripped into the man to tear large holes and almost shred him, but he simply stood and took the shots as blinding red-orange light surrounded his body. The magical pressure from the building energy turned her stomach.

This isn't good.

Her eyes widened, and she thrust upward, released her

shadow blades, and forced all her energy into her wings. More than anything, she needed speed.

She stared into the sky and focused on nothing more than rocketing away from the ground as fast as she could manage.

The revenant exploded and released a massive pulse of energy. The blast obliterated nearby trees and set several on fire. She continued her upward flight as the shockwave crashed into the remaining attackers.

Long moments passed before she dared looked down. She took a deep breath. A cloud of debris grew almost like a tree in fast-forward below her.

He didn't have to do that. We could have won.

Alison recharged her shields and squinted before she floated cautiously lower as the debris cloud finished its growth and began to collapse. A crater gaped where the revenant had once been.

Two dark figures moved on the ground, covered in ash, dirt, and mud. One sparked from several joints in the armor.

Her nostrils flared, and she soared toward the figure in the sparking power armor, gliding on her wings. She fused her shadow blades into a long shadow lance.

The men's deflectors were shattered, and only small remnants were left of the armor. Their thrust packs had been twisted by the flames. Their armor itself was pitted and melted which made their movements awkward. It was a miracle they hadn't been killed instantly in such a massive explosion.

Nice tech. Too bad it won't save you now.

Her lance pierced the center of the armor. She released

the energy and vaulted back to summon two shadow blades. The man turned to fire at her with a machine gun, but the half-melted slag was no longer useful as a weapon.

Alison barked out a laugh. "Too bad, asshole. I'm scratched up with a few burns here and there, and you have nothing. Did I also mention I'm pissed off?"

Her adversary backed away, the movements unsteady from both the damage and the uneven topography of the rough crater.

She pointed her blade at the man as ash, rock, and dirt continued to rain down around her. "Get out right now. Considering you and your friends tried to kill me, I have every right to kill you. I'll give you this one last chance to surrender, if only because I have a few questions. But if you try something, you won't live to regret it."

He stopped moving. A moment later, the back opened, and the bloodied operator slid out, his jumpsuit burned and torn. He walked out with his hands above his head and a slight frown on his face.

"I've cleared the rest of the enemies," Alison reported. "The revenant killed himself."

No one responded. She tapped her ear. The receiver was still in place.

Maybe there was some sort of EMP from the blast or these guys have some other source of jamming. It doesn't matter for now.

She marched over to her captive. "I don't know what your exact orders were, but did they include the damned words, 'Kill Alison Brownstone?'"

The wounded man swallowed. "We had orders to neutralize the project. You shouldn't have been involved.

There was some...confusion during our initial deployment. I'm sorry for the accidental attack. The primary mission has always been to kill the project."

"Accidental attack?" She put the blade to his throat. "Those were some rather specific accidents that happened. Now, who the hell are you? You're obviously not military or any type of AET, but you have some damned fancy gear."

"Why should I tell you anything?" the man sneered, and his earlier fear had vanished completely from his face.

This asshole seriously thinks he has the upper hand?

Alison stared at him, stunned by his brashness. "For starters, because I have a shadow blade to your throat? But, sure, go on. Keep trying my patience after you tried to kill me."

He shook his head. "You won't execute a prisoner. We know all about you."

She lowered her blade and shook her head. "But you accidentally attacked me? Do you expect me to believe that?"

The man's face twitched. "I'll admit mistakes were made."

As in, 'We mistakenly didn't kill you right away.'

"If you try anything, it'd be self-defense, not executing a prisoner." She released the shadow blade. "And you know I've killed many people I thought had it coming."

He nodded slowly and seemed a little uncertain.

"So, here's how this will go, asshole," she explained. "Very soon, my friends will arrive. One of them is my over-protective ex-bodyguard life wizard boyfriend. Another is a former dark witch assassin, and the third is a nine-tailed fox who can charm people and get them to do things they would never think of doing." She offered him a thin smile. "And they're all probably seriously pissed that they didn't get to join the fun, but they can have fun interrogating you. Think of the different methods they'll be able to try, and you have to ask yourself, 'What good will holding onto this information actually do me?'"

"You're saying you would let them torture me?"

Alison let the threat hang in the air. Hana's powers were hardly torture, but the implication of other more painful methods might be enough to get the man to crack.

"It's been that kind of month," she suggested.

"You wouldn't allow that. That's not how you work." He definitely sounded uncertain now.

She released her wings but didn't bother to heal her wounds. For the moment, she wanted to feel some of the pain. It was very clarifying.

"I was getting through to him." She gestured around the crater and at the collapsed trees. "I stopped him from killing those campers, and I was talking to the man underneath, but then you assholes showed up." She glared at him. "So don't sit there smug in the knowledge of what you think you know about me. Think about what I did to Derek Chesterton, Scott Carlyle, and the Eastern Union." Her face twitched. "Think about what I did to the damned Seventh Order," she shouted. "Just because I'm not my father doesn't mean I don't have my limits. Understand, asshole?"

The man flinched.

Alison took a few deep breaths. "Now, let's try this again. Who do you work for? Keep in mind, even if you think you can stonewall here and somehow, none of my friends pull it out of you painfully or otherwise, you're not going anywhere. I'm taking your DNA, and my infomancer will find out who you are in an hour. Refusing will accomplish nothing other than angering me."

He sighed and raised his head as he tried for a defiant look. "I work for a private military contracting firm. New Century Tactical Solutions."

She frowned. While she'd vaguely heard of NCTS, she hadn't run across them in a job before. With so many PMC firms, ranging from barely concealed murder squads to highly professional and respectable organizations, it was too difficult to keep track.

"And what were your exact orders?" she asked.

"To find and engage the project and eliminate him." The man looked around the crater. "Technically, the project's eliminated." He looked thoughtful. Maybe he thought he could claim the money all for himself.

"He wasn't a project. He was a man. He had a name." Alison sighed. She didn't even know the man's name.

The mercenary shrugged. "A job's a job. It's not like that guy wasn't dangerous."

He's dangerous because they made him dangerous.

"Who was your client?" she demanded.

"Look, I don't know. You can do whatever you want to me, and you'll find out that's true. I simply follow my orders. I'm the wrong guy to ask about who is paying the checks. NCTS doesn't work that way."

"And were your orders to kill me, too? And how did you find him anyway?"

The mercenary took a deep breath, the calculation

obvious on his face. "You led us to him, and no, we didn't have orders to kill you."

Alison narrowed her eyes. "You had orders to kill any witnesses, didn't you?"

He swallowed but didn't deny it. He must have been too afraid to risk a lie. "We knew to search the area, and when we found out there was someone else here, we decided to see if you had any luck. We thought the people we tailed might wound the project and soften him up for us. When we followed you, we didn't know it was you exactly. Nobody said anything about Alison Brownstone being here."

She scoffed. "I'm only a concerned citizen, asshole."

"Sure. Same here." The man licked his lips. "Now, since you didn't kill me, I'll do you a favor. You think we only have two dropships and six armored men? We knew how tough that guy might be, and I don't think you're in any position to take on any reinforcements." He smiled. "I noticed you tapping that receiver in your ear. Are you having any comms trouble? Did you wonder why that is?"

"Oh, I know exactly why it is. Don't feel so smug." She laughed. "And you're seriously trying to intimidate me? Oh, I get it. You tried to stall because you hoped your reinforcements would come and save you. There's one problem with that. My reinforcements are coming sooner."

They both locked eyes and waited as they took shallow breaths. Neither said a word. It was time to see which side won the race.

A couple of minutes later, two blurs emerged from the tree line and stopped at the top of the crater. They resolved into a scowling Mason and a red-skinned glowing fox woman with nine tails and a large sword. A moment later, Drysi burst out of the trees and halted beside the others.

The trio bounded down the crater toward Alison and her prisoner.

She nodded toward her friends. "Are you ready to take on the entire Brownstone Security primary field team?"

The mercenary's shoulders slumped.

She stared at him for a moment and scoffed. "You don't have any reinforcements, do you? Nice try." She shook her head. "You know what, asshole? Enjoy your walk back." She started up the crater. "Let's get the hell out of here."

She stopped at the top of the ridge and stared down into the center. At least the revenant wouldn't threaten anyone ever again.

I hope you finally found peace.

CHAPTER TWENTY-THREE

A few days later, Alison folded her arms over her chest as she frowned at Agent Latherby behind his desk. She'd fielded a few questions from the media after the campers had reported what had happened, but she'd avoided attention as much as she could, unsure how the agent wanted to handle it. To her surprise, he sent her a brief message and told her to go ahead and tell people she had been doing contract work for the PDA.

Today's meeting was the first face-to-face encounter since before he had sent her after the revenant.

"I'm sorry, Miss Brownstone," the agent explained quietly. "I didn't tell you that before, so I wanted to tell you now. I miscalculated badly. I won't make any excuses other than noting I learn from mistakes. I didn't understand much about what was going on. I hope you can accept my sincere apology for what it is and especially for my assurance that you wouldn't have to deal with additional forces, which complicated matters."

"I don't blame you, and I know you weren't trying to set me up." She sighed and nodded. "It is what it is, and I might not have been able to save him anyway, even if the NCTS assholes hadn't shown up. What about the other things I asked about? You said you only wanted to talk about them in person."

Agent Latherby nodded. "I've sent some information on to Senator Johnston per your request and a few other contacts of my own. We'll see what happens in the next few days, but unfortunately for whoever tried to cover this up, the massive explosion made it difficult, if not impossible."

"Are you sure? I know there are some impressive cover-ups out there."

She wondered how much he knew about the Battle of L.A. He'd implied several times he knew more about her father than most people, but he'd never flat-out stated he understood his true history.

"That's true," Agent Latherby responded, "but it doesn't change the fact that this cover-up is failing. They tried to push a story of a mini-eruption from a somehow previously unknown volcanic vent and passively mentioned magic might be involved. No one is buying it, however, if only because Johnston and many of his allies are making sure they don't. That's the key to a good cover-up, Miss Brownstone. It has to have considerable buy-in from powerful people, or it fails. This is one secret that won't stay secret. There will be many hearings and investigations in the coming months."

"I never cared about covering it up, you know." Alison shrugged. "I simply wanted to make sure innocent people weren't hurt. I'm not a government agent, so I don't care about preserving its reputation."

"I do care about our reputation, but I also prioritize the protection of the lives of American citizens." He took a deep breath. "I've also found out a few things about Project Revenant. I don't know if it means anything to you, but the man was actually a volunteer in a certain sense. I don't think it makes it any better, but at least they didn't pluck a man off the street."

She shook her head. "There's no way in hell anyone would volunteer to be turned into that. I could see it if he didn't know what he was, but he knew."

The agent nodded. "In a strict sense, you're right. I don't know the name of the man, but he was a former special forces soldier who had previously signed a document wherein he agreed that should he be mortally injured and there weren't magical healing resources otherwise available, they could harvest his body for experimental magical healing research. It'll be a long time before the armed forces can have a healing potion for every soldier or a life wizard in every unit."

"Those sons of bitches. That wasn't magical healing." Alison curled her hands into fists. "I'm telling you right now. If the system can't handle it, I'll handle it. I don't want these people to get away with this crap, and I won't let them. I might not be some high-powered politician, but being the Dark Princess has to be good for something other than scaring criminals."

"Give it some time, Miss Brownstone. I think the system can work in this case." Agent Latherby folded his hands in front of him. "And also keep in mind, I bucked my own people to bring you in on this. There's already strong evidence that a senior PDA official might have been involved. The agency will have a big black eye."

"Some things can't be allowed," she seethed. "Some things are wrong, no matter who is doing them."

"I know. I agree." He frowned. "And I'm disturbed by not only that but also the fact that the NCTS showed up. They are the very definition of mercenary scum, and I presume you, like me, don't believe for a second that they attacked you accidentally. Again, I miscalculated and involved you in something even more corrupt than I anticipated. I believe some players wanted to take their opportunity to rid themselves of a Brownstone as they see you as a threat to their plans."

"And now? Will they come after me? If so, I'll simply add them to the list, but it'll be nice to be prepared. Maybe I can make T-shirts to give to people. 'I tried to assassinate Alison Brownstone, and all I got was this lousy T-Shirt.'"

Agent Latherby shook his head, a faint look of approval in his eyes. "I've already put feelers out, and I know certain high-level politicians support you, not only Senator Johnston. Those on the other side might want to press the issue to try to make you look bad, but many of them are about to find themselves out of a job. While not all members of their factions will likely be purged, they probably won't mess with you again because everyone knows what happens if you keep going after a Brownstone. Your recent performance in Vancouver was a strong reminder of that for everyone."

"They probably won't come after me?" Alison asked.

He shrugged. "Some people are stupid. What can I say?"

She chuckled. "That they are, Agent Latherby. That they are."

CHAPTER TWENTY-FOUR

Alison smiled as she stared at her phone. She sat in bed, waiting for Mason, when an alarm went off. She'd had Tahir set up some special news alerts for her, but she hadn't expected them to activate so soon.

"That's what I wanted to see." She closed her eyes and took a deep breath. "I haven't been this satisfied since Scott was convicted."

Mason slipped into the bed, the spicy scent of his after-shave hanging in the air. "What's got you smiling so much, A? I'm not complaining, but you were down the last few days."

She turned the phone to show him the headline. "I had an early Christmas gift, and it didn't involve me having to beat anyone else up."

"FRANKENSTEIN" SHOCKER! FOUR-STAR GENERAL AND SENIOR PDA OFFICIAL INDICTED AS PART OF INVESTIGATION INTO ILLEGAL "PROJECT REVENANT"

Side-by-side images of the general and official being arrested and led away in cuffs sat below the headline.

Alison grinned like a teen given their first car. "I honestly didn't think it would happen so quickly. I'd half-decided they would start an investigation, drag their feet, find a few low-level peons to throw on the sacrificial pyre, and go home to start a new version of the project. I know there are more people involved out there, but they got the top of the chain, and that's some justice."

"They couldn't let this drag out. Even some of the guys who might be on their side wouldn't hold back." He shrugged. "Too many investigations could cause a ton of trouble, and certain people were waiting for an opportunity to headhunt, but it's good to see the bastards get what they deserve."

"Exactly. I already wondered if I could investigate it myself. This saves me the trouble." She nodded as satisfying warmth suffused her body. A perp-walk for the people involved was almost as good as sex with Mason. Maybe better.

I'd better not tell him that.

Alison snickered.

"What's so funny?" Mason asked.

"Nothing. I thought about the guys being arrested."

That was close.

He laughed. "I'm glad it didn't end up Brownstone Security against the Department of Defense and the Paranormal Defense Agency. I think that's a fight even we can't win." He thought it over for a second. "If we added your Dad and Izzie, we probably could."

She laughed. "Yeah. No wonder they're so freaked by us."

At some point, I'll have to tell him the truth about Dad. He already knows the truth about Mom. I should ask Dad first, though.

Alison turned her phone off and set it on her nightstand. "This has been a crazy month. Helping mobsters, your ex-girlfriend, and having some Drow princess wanting to be my bestie would have been a lot, even without Project Revenant."

"Isn't every month a crazy month for us?" he asked with a smile. "It's not like people hire Brownstone Security to help protect school bake sales."

"This has been maybe not the craziest ever, but definitely in the top." She lowered her head to her pillow. "And it makes me think."

"Think about what?"

She shrugged. "I wonder a lot about my entire first year in Seattle and about the impact I've made since moving here. I never had the kind of relationship with D.C. that I have with this city."

"What about it?" Mason lay down and rolled to face his girlfriend. Even the glories of his pecs and abs on full display weren't enough to distract her from her introspection.

"I want to make this city a better place," Alison explained. "And I keep asking myself—have I made it a better place or simply a more scared place? I don't want to end up making more trouble for people."

He scoffed. "A, crime is down and the bad guys are

running scared, but normal people aren't. They're happy. And think about Scott Carlyle. By taking down him alone, you helped save millions of people from a painful disease and probably stopped an eventual civil war. Yeah, you've knocked heads here and there, but you've also always given people a chance, which is why Hana and Drysi both work for you now. Imagine where they would have ended up without you."

Alison sighed. Hana had been on a path toward a very bad place, and Drysi had barely pulled herself out of a pit of total corruption.

Her boyfriend shrugged. "I don't know if I would be able to do that, but you've turned a con artist and a dark wizard assassin into protectors of the people, and don't forget the Mountain Strider. Even if the military could have dealt with it, that thing would have killed thousands of people before they did. Have you had a positive impact on Seattle? You're damned right you've had a positive impact on Seattle, and this is a much better place now because you moved here and made it that way."

"So much has happened in such a short time. Kind of the same thing happened to my dad and mom. Their lives were stable in their own ways, and then everything changed, and so much happened in a short time." She smiled. "Thanks, Mason, I needed that."

"I know." He grinned. "I think it's your Brownstone way of keeping yourself from getting a swelled head, but sometimes, you could benefit from it."

"You think so?" Alison reached over to stroke his cheek. "I don't know if I need to have a big ego as long as I have the world's most handsome hype-man."

Mason leaned over and kissed her forehead. "I'll always be here for you, A. I love you. Always remember that."

"I love you, too, Mason." She stifled a laugh.

"What?"

"I was thinking that of course you'll always be here for me. We live together now." She released the full laugh. "And you're even fairly good at remembering the toilet seat."

He grinned. "I do try. It's a difficult challenge, but I'm sure I'll eventually conquer it."

"So, uh, while we're on the subject of relationships..." she began and fluttered her eyelashes in mock innocence.

Here we go. I don't think he'll have a problem with what I'm about to ask, but you never know. Some days, it really sucks not having soul sight anymore.

"What?" He eyed her with suspicion. "Why are you giving me that look? It's a very Hana look."

Alison snickered. "A Hana look?"

He shrugged. "Kind of. It has me worried."

"Easy question first. I assume you're still okay to go down to L.A. for Christmas?"

Mason nodded. "That's fine. I know your dad likes me more now, even if he won't always show it, and it'll be interesting to spend more time around them on their turf instead of ours. I think I can score points with your dad by eating at his restaurant."

"Most definitely, and you're right about him liking you. Yeah, that came up when I talked to him a while back. I think Vancouver was the big turning point, even if he tolerated you before, that convinced him." Alison sucked in a long, deep breath. "There was something else he mentioned during that conversation that I hadn't thought about, but it was a good idea. I wanted to bring it up with you and see what you think."

"What's that?" He looked more curious than suspicious now. "And does it involve barbecue?"

"No, no barbecue." She sat up and smiled. "It's simpler than that. You've met my parents, but I've never met yours, and I think it's about time I do."

He nodded slowly. "True, and fair enough." He took a deep breath.

Alison laughed. "You suddenly look nervous. Do you think your parents will hate me?"

"When I met your dad, he tried to shame me for not having killed any three-headed dragons." Mason shrugged. "You never know what will happen with parents. I think they'll like you, but they're also very different from your parents and you might have trouble relating to them. They still don't understand why I didn't become a healer, and I'm their son."

"If I can take on a Drow princess, I can meet with my boyfriend's parents." She winked. "And I haven't killed any three-headed dragons or healed any of them."

"And does it mean anything, A?" His expression grew serious. "The fact that you want to meet my parents?"

She leaned forward to give him a soft kiss. "To get to any destination, you have to take steps along the way. The steps aren't the final part, but they definitely have meaning."

A huge smile settled over his face. "Meeting my parents can definitely be arranged. Does sometime after Christmas sound good?"

"It sounds good to me." Alison lay down again.

"Assuming the other three Drow princesses don't try to kill me, Omni doesn't turn out to be some evil demon sent to destroy Earth, the Mountain Strider doesn't wake up, some monster doesn't burst out of Mt. St. Helens, and Mom doesn't suddenly get some super-rare craving that forces me to scour the Earth and Oriceran to save Dad from a life of eternal suffering at the hands of a pregnant woman who happens to be super-deadly."

Mason shook his head. "Don't worry. I'm sure only one of those things will happen in the next few months. Two, tops." He grinned.

"You know what?" She laughed. "I shouldn't have opened a security company. I should have simply opened my own sushi place."

The story is far from over. Alison's adventure continues in <u>A BROWNSTONE SOLUTION</u>

FREE BOOKS!

WARNING:

The Troll is now in charge.

And he's giving away free books
if you sign-up!

Join the only newsletter hosted by a Troll!

Get sneak peeks, exclusive giveaways, behind the scenes
content, and more.
PLUS you'll be notified of special **one day only fan
pricing** on new releases.

CLICK HERE

or visit: https://marthacarr.com/read-free-stories/

The story is far from over. Alison's adventure continues in A BROWNSTONE SOLUTION

AVAILABLE FOR PURCHASE HERE

For Hire: Teachers for special school in Virginia countryside.

Must be able to handle teenagers with special abilities.

Cannot be afraid to discipline werewolves, wizards, elves and other assorted hormonal teens.

Apply at the School of Necessary Magic.

AVAILABLE AT AMAZON RETAILERS

I'm up to something new in indie author land. No surprise if you've been hanging around these stories for a while. I've been wanting to create a bigger experience for readers beyond just a Facebook group (The Peabrain Society – if you're not in there yet, it's a lot of fun), and really great stories.

That's a lot... but what if it could be more? Frankly, the family that's been created in the group is what's helped inspire what's coming next.

The idea is something I've been carrying around in my back pocket for a while looking for the right team members to grow it into something real. I can't say too much just yet... the big reveal is coming in just a couple of months. Meanwhile, there's a lot of busy bees working alongside me to get the thing rolling because there's a lot of moving parts.

Our goal is to create new ways you can immerse yourself in a world of magic even more, and at the same time go for your own dreams, but with a twist. What if you had some guidance that helped figure out the rough patches and a lot of other people cheering you on when things were going great?

It'd be a lot easier, maybe even doable. Frankly, it's what I've found to be the case. I was working in a vacuum as an author for years till I ran into Michael Anderle. These days it's a village and a lot more fun. Sure, it's remote but imagine having a team of people to ask for referrals or share a joke or keep time writing away, knowing someone else is doing the same. It's so much easier.

Instead of trying to build a pool of knowledge based off just my experience, I can dip into this pool and get some answers, skipping a lot of expensive steps. And I can do the same for others.

What if we could all do that for each other... in general, all the time in a more structured way that actually lead somewhere? I've been mentoring young women for years and over time have put together a series of things that have helped all of us move forward into lives beyond what we were wishing for – that's real magic.

And it's that encouragement I keep getting to reach out to a wider audience that's gotten me to jumpstart this idea. More will be coming, including how to join in so be thinking about what your big dream is – this isn't about flashy (unless that's your thing), this is all about the personal – big or small. And in a couple months, we'll get rolling and reveal it all. Stay tuned, more adventures to follow (lots more).

THANK YOU for not only reading this story but these *Author Notes* as well.

(I think I've been good with always opening with "thank you." If not, I need to edit the other *Author Notes*!)

RANDOM (*sometimes*) THOUGHTS?

WOOT!

Did you see that we have an Unbelievable Mister Brownstone Book 19?

Oh, you thought since James was married and retired that he would just go off into the sunset, didn't you?

HA!

We have him coming back for just 4 more stories, ones we like to think of as the BBQ Road Trip stories. Ok, maybe that's just me that likes to think of them that way but I get to put BBQ into the stories, just saying.

Because sometimes the wife just wants the husband to get out of the house and go do something…anything…

Not that my wife has EVER said anything remotely like that about me and you should totally believe me.

Because I'm an author - and I make up stories for a living

AROUND THE WORLD IN 80 DAYS

One of the interesting (at least to me) aspects of my life is the ability to work from anywhere and at any time. In the future, I hope to re-read my own *Author Notes* and remember my life as a diary entry.

Cave in the Sky(™), Las Vegas Nv USA

The time is 7:27 AM in the morning, I've been up for two (2) hours and now I need a Coke, *STAT!*

(Stat means really quick, right? Damn, now I need to go look it up.)

From medicinenet.com: STAT: *A common medical abbreviation for urgent or rush. From the Latin word statum, meaning 'immediately.'*

Ok good, I'm using it correctly. These are the things that I occasionally know I have right, but then doubt starts to creep into my brain imagining all of the horrible situations where me using the term wrong could show up in a future interview.

Finally, my brain starts to relax when I remember this is going through Lynne's capable editing hands and she would have calmly fixed my 'oops' without me being any wiser.

Bless Editors around the world, they help fix creative screw-ups and make stories so much better for readers.

FAN PRICING

$0.99 Saturdays (new LMBPN stuff) and $0.99 Wednesday (both LMBPN books and friends of LMBPN books.) Get great stuff from us and others at tantalizing prices.

Go ahead, I bet you can't read just one.

Sign up here: http://lmbpn.com/email/.

HOW TO MARKET FOR BOOKS YOU LOVE

Review them so others have your thoughts, tell friends and the dogs of your enemies (because who wants to talk with enemies?)... *Enough said ;-)*

Ad Aeternitatem,

Michael Anderle

JOIN THE ORICERAN UNIVERSE FAN GROUP ON FACEBOOK!

CONNECT WITH THE AUTHORS

Martha Carr Social

Website: http://www.marthacarr.com

Facebook: https://www.facebook.com/
groups/MarthaCarrFans/

Michael Anderle Social

Michael Anderle Social
Website:
http://www.lmbpn.com

Email List:
http://lmbpn.com/email/

Facebook Here: https://www.
facebook.com/TheKurtherianGambitBooks/